To Michelle for her love ... ...ence and Josh, Laurie, Oliver and Charlotte for inspiring me every day.

To Fiona

Best wishes

Josh

"Lest we forget"

RUDYARD KIPLING

CONTENTS

Epigraph..3
 CHAPTER ONE: 3
CHAPTER TWO:..3
CHAPTER THREE: 3
CHAPTER FOUR: 3
CHAPTER FIVE: 3
CHAPTER SIX: 3
CHAPTER SEVEN: 3
CHAPTER EIGHT: 3
CHAPTER NINE: 3
CHAPTER TEN: 3
CHAPTER ELEVEN: 3
CHAPTER TWELVE: 3
CHAPTER THIRTEEN: 3
CHAPTER FOURTEEN: 3
CHAPTER FIFTEEN: 3
CHAPTER SIXTEEN: 3
CHAPTER SEVENTEEN:..3
CHAPTER EIGHTEEN: 3
Dedication...1

BUGLE BOY
By Jonathan Jones

© Jonathan Jones 2023

CHAPTER ONE:

Spring 1912

"Finger, thumb or rusty bum?"

Harry Jones rounded the corner into the play- ground and hurried towards the heap of struggling boys. This was one of his favourite games and he wasn't going to miss out. He was almost upon them and was about to shout "Bagsy Topsies!" to make sure he was on the team jumping onto the other lads' backs when Foxy's mean face grinned up at him from the middle of the pile. Harry's heart sank. Foxy had teased and bullied him since he was little and today was no different.

"Hey up it's that laddy-lass I want hold of," he said as he stood up brushing the dust from his shorts and stockings. Harry was never quite sure if he was kidding or not as his thin face held the same slightly sneering expression most of the time and it was impossible to gauge his mood though it was usually mean.

"All right Foxy," he mumbled, "what you lakin'?"

He felt small and stupid straight away; it was obvious what they were playing and he'd gone and asked a silly question.

"We're doing a music hall act who do you want to be, Marie Lloyd or Little Titch?"

The bigger boy sneered and all the others laughed, even his best mate, George, Harry noticed.

"I mean, I know you're playing rusty bum, but what are t'teams?"

"You can be on our team," said George, "but you'll have to be post."

"All right, I'll just put this safe," Harry said, placing a small maroon case up against the wall.

"What you got there?" Foxy asked.

"It's my cornet, I'm on my way to band practice"

"What's tha mean, "cornet"? Tha can't keep ice cream in a box."

This was Foxy's joke every time he saw Harry on his way to rehearsal and he never tired of it. He looked around at the other lads, daring them not to laugh and eliciting some sycophantic sniggers.

"Give us a go on it!"

"I can't," Harry said, "it cost a packet and my dad would go mad"

"Poor little laddy lass is yitten," Foxy sneered, looking round at the rest of them again.

"He isn't scared of you Foxy, it's his dad, he's massive! Have you seen him?" George said quickly, "He could paste you."

"Massive? Tell us another, he's a squirt like Jonesy. He's nowt and if he touched me, my pa would kill him, he's twice his size and he's twice as hard."

Harry reached to pick his cornet case up but it was too late, Foxy's thumbs were already at work unspringing the shiny brass clips on the case.

"I bet I can play a tune! What shall I give you? How about "When Father Painted The Parlour"?"

He lifted the beautiful, shiny cornet to his mouth.

"Where's tha blow?"

"Well here's a clue, it isn't the big end."

The boys all laughed, including George who also sneaked a quick glance at Harry as if to say, "Still your mate, sorry about before."

Foxy stared at Harry for a moment a look of puzzlement on his face, then joined in the laughter, he could always thump him later Then he raised the cornet again. Harry saw he hadn't attached the mouthpiece and had a little smile to himself; this would be good!

Foxy put the narrow tube to his mouth and blew as hard as he could; there was the slightly amplified sound of rushing air, but nothing resembling a note. He tried again and this time there came a sharp, high pitched farting sound. There was a shocked silence for a second then the lads burst into hysterical laughter, hanging onto each other and staggering around,

"Again! Do it again Foxy," someone shouted above the racket.

"Again, again!"

It took him three attempts between fits of giggles before he managed it but eventually, there it was, the same revolting noise as before. The lads reeled around, holding their noses and wafting their hands in front of their faces, shouting "You dirty get," at each other and pretending to pass out from the imaginary smell.

"Give us it back then," Harry said after a while.

"Only if you play us a tune," a scruffy, dishevelled looking lad called Douglas shouted. He was laughing so hard that a great bubble of snot billowed from his nose which he wiped away on the sleeve of his jacket. His little round glasses which were held together on the bridge with fuse wire had slipped down and he squinched them back up with a wrinkle of his nose.

"Yeah, play us a tune," said George and all the boys began to chant,

"Play us a tune, play us a tune, play us a tune!"

"All right, all right, I will if you want," said Harry holding his hands palm upwards in front of them to quell the noise. He put his hand out for his cornet and after hanging onto it for longer than was necessary, Foxy handed it over.

Harry made a great show of taking the mouthpiece from its little compartment in the case and attaching it carefully. He was hoping Foxy would feel stupid but when he looked at him there was nothing to show that he did; his long thin face was as blank as a piece of paper which was a pleasant change from the usual sneer.

He put the cornet to his lips and blew a long, clear note that cut through the late afternoon air like a blade of ice, then he ran out a series of scales and arpeggios as fast as he could, his fingers moving impossibly fast on the little pearl topped valves. The other boys stared; it seemed impossible to play so loud and so long without taking a breath. When he finished the lads cheered in delight but Foxy wasn't impressed.

"Very good Jonesy, but we said a tune not just some racket"
"Just warming up, Foxy, just warming up," Harry said. He felt in command now, this was his world and Foxy couldn't touch it.
He began to play "Who Were You With Last Night?" in a jaunty, lively style and after a couple of bars the gang of lads began to clap along ; he even spotted one or two toes beginning to tap in time. He felt very daring because he'd been clipped round the ear by his dad

when he'd dared to play it at home. He didn't really know why but his dad seemed to think it was "A filthy little ditty"

He whipped through the chorus, the notes trilling and tumbling like a fall of clear, cold, bubbling water until he came to the end and finished with a flourish of double tongued fancy work that had the lads whooping in amazement.

"That were blooming great Harry! You're reight good on it, I wish I could learn summat like that," said Stanley, a tall, gentle looking lad in a torn gansey whose stockings were always wrinkled round his ankles, "it were reight loud though, you've nearly busted me ear 'oles." He wiggled his fingers in his ears for emphasis and grinned. "You should be on at Attercliffe Palace, you'd earn a packet!"

"Smashing," agreed George turning to the rest of them, "I told you he was good didn't I?" There was a bit of reflected glory being Harry's mate and George felt a little knot of pride in his chest.

"Come on, let's play rusty bum," Harry said quickly. He didn't really like this praise and he was also sure Foxy was going to come out with some smart Alec response before long. He walked over to the little maroon case and taking care to blow out the spit from its little valve, he placed the cornet back in its plush interior, closing the clips with a satisfying click. He loved the thought of it lying there in the dark just waiting to come back to life in his hands. Sometimes he thought he didn't need anything else in the world to make him happy except his mum, his dad, his brother and his cornet.

"I'm post!" he shouted and took up his position facing the wall with his arms outstretched and his palms flat against it. He felt arms come around his waist and a shoulder was pressed firmly into his kidneys. He glanced over his shoulder and saw the rest of his team doubling over and joining onto each other in a line like carriages in a train jamming their shoulders against the thighs of the lads in front and grabbing hold of a fistful of jersey to stay steady like rugby players in a scrum. He braced himself as the first lad in the other team began his run up. The idea was to leapfrog as far as you could down the line so it was a good tactic to use your lightest lad first. Little Tommy Smith was scampering towards his target with a look of fierce determination on his grubby pink face. He landed with a hefty thud and Harry was pushed uncomfortably close to the wall.

"One up!" shouted Tommy and the next lad began to run. When they were all aboard and the lads underneath were groaning beneath their combined weight the last lad held his fist aloft with the thumb sticking up and shouted "Finger, thumb or rusty bum?"

There was a quick mutter of discussion among the boys underneath and they shouted out their guess, "Rusty bum!" meaning a clenched fist with the thumb tucked in.

" Ha Ha ! wrong !" shouted the riders, "it were thumb ! Our jump again !"

The boys underneath buckled on purpose and the whole lot of them collapsed in a dusty, struggling, giggling heap before forming up again with a new boy as post and Harry at the far end of the caterpillar ready for the next leap.

It was a sweaty, tired Harry who trotted down Wheel Lane to the band room in the "Four Square Gospellers" chapel and he could hear the other lads warming up as he passed the open window and pushed open the door.

"Tha late!" murmered John Fenwick as Harry unfolded his wooden chair and sat down hastily.

"I know, sorry. I wa' playing rusty bum and forgot t'time."

"Tha'll lose thi seat, cornet players are ten a penny tha knows. Not worth losing it for a kid's game."

"I know, but are they as good as me?" Harry thought. He'd never have said it out loud because his dad had instilled it in him that you had to believe in yourself in your head whilst being humble and polite in public but he knew it to be true.

"Did tha win?

"Eh?"

"Rusty bum! Did tha win?"

Harry was miles away and it took him a moment to understand, "Oh, sorry, no we didn't because Foxy kept cheating. Even their team told us he had after we'd finished."

"Why didn't they tell you before?" John asked

"Because they're all scared of him that's why!"

"Why? He's nowt him!"

"He is if you're me," said Harry to himself.

"Hey up, he's here!" John said, having a final waggle of his instrument's valves.

The conductor, Mr Barnes was a kindly middle aged man with a soft smiling face but he was a tartar if you weren't concentrating so, as he tapped on his music stand with his ivory baton, there was absolute silence. The lads wondered about this baton because once he had tapped the stand Mr Barnes always slipped it back into its little red, silk lined box, carefully put it in his jacket pocket and conducted for the rest of the practice with his hands.

"Right boys, The Old Rugged Cross."

There was rustle of shuffled sheet music on stands then at the conductor's down stroke the old hymn tune rose and swelled and all thoughts of Foxy vanished from Harry's mind as he concentrated on the music in front of him.

He sauntered up through the village enjoying the mild, purpling twilight redolent with the scents of summer gardens. The barley fields were still green and the occasional gentle breeze sent waves across them making them look like great sheets of softly billowing velvet. He paused to watch bats dance around a just lit gas lamp where tiny insects whirled, so it was dusk when Harry got home. The kitchen door was open when he walked up the path. He shouted a quick hello to his mum who was sitting on a kitchen chair close to the door wafting cool air over herself with a newspaper, then ran upstairs to the bedroom he shared with his brother Laurie. He pulled open the top drawer of his dresser and rooted about among the assorted bits of junk a boy of his age collects until he found what he was looking for; a little cream coloured ceramic pot containing a waxy balm called Arnica. He scooped a little dollop onto his finger and gently smeared it over his lips. After a moment's discomfort a warm soothing feeling began to spread and his bruised lips tingled rather than hurt. Mr Barnes had recommended the stuff and said no cornet player should ever be without it. Protecting your lip and developing a true embouchure was key to being a top player and Harry was determined to be just that no matter how much it hurt.

A door banged downstairs and Harry heard his dad's voice rumbling in the kitchen. This was his favourite time of the day. Harry's dad was a steel worker and had been from the age of fourteen and Harry idolised him. He'd once visited the works with his pa and seen the crucibles of white hot molten metal being poured into moulds, spitting and sparking in the gloom of the shopfloor and burning black marks into the men's heavy leather aprons. Some of them even did it bare chested but his pa said they were fools. He'd been in awe of his dad's bravery ever since. He seemed so casual, occasionally grunting as he flicked a dot of glowing steel from his brawny forearm when a splash leapt from the lip of the vessel. Harry could smell the acrid stink of sizzling hair causing him to wrinkle his nose. "Doesn't it hurt?" he'd asked. His dad had raised an eyebrow and said, "Not if you're quick lad; it's a bit like them fakirs who can walk on hot coals, if you brush it off quick it doesn't have a chance to burn you." Nonetheless Harry had seen the little blue/black scars where his dad hadn't been quick enough and thought he was tough and brave. In two years Harry would be joining him in the steel works if he had his way and felt a thrill of excitement to think that he might be that casual about the dangerous world of white hot molten metal and crashing machinery.

CHAPTER TWO:

February 2016

A mizzle of fine rain was falling, threatening to turn to sleet as Chris talked quietly to the group of children gathered in the "Dud Corner" cemetery near the village of Loos-en-Gohelle in Northern France. Chris was an excellent guide who had gone out of his way to find personal stories to interest the pupils who were on a four day visit to the battlefields of The Great War. They were looking at a freshly turfed, narrow grave with a sparkling white Portland Stone headstone bearing the inscription, "A soldier of The Great War, Yorks and Lancs regiment, Known Unto God"

It had been an emotional day; a cold day which seemed to match the sombre mood. Earlier, Chris had taken them to the great monument to the lost of the Somme at Thiepval and among the seventy thousand or more names one of the lads had found the name of his great great uncle.

"I knew it were there," he'd said, "but I didn't think I'd find it"

He was a big tough lad, Richard but his eyes had filled with tears and he'd grunted, "Need a fag," The teachers exchanged a look then decided to let him go.

He stood on a far corner of the monument, smoking and a small man in an ill fitting uniform stood alongside him, muddy but cheerful,

"Go twos with you?" he said, "got a big push later and I dropped me fags through the duck boards! Could reight do wi'one." He pushed his tin hat back and winked, his bushy moustache tilting as he grinned and held his hand out. Richard turned, offering his half smoked cigarette but through tears which made his sight wobble he saw of course that the little soldier was not there.

Mr Jones' voice called, "Ok Rich?"

"Yeah, yeah, sorry, all a bit much that," he called back.

"Now we don't know exactly who he was," said Chris, "but we know a fair bit about him from his remains. First we know from his cap badge he was from the 12th Yorks and Lancs regiment or Sheffield Pals battalion. We also know from research that he was just a lad, probably about fourteen or fifteen years of age." He paused to let that horrifying fact sink in a little.

"Same age as most of us," someone muttered, "bloody hell."

"And finally, we know why he was there," Chris said.

He reached into a duffel bag he had brought to the graveside and there was an audible gasp which sent plumes of silver breath into the cold air as he unwrapped a battered and flattened bugle from its yellow lint covering.

" He was a bugle boy. This bugle is going to be exhibited in the Imperial War Museum in London but I have been allowed to show it to you as a very special favour; it's a very rare object."

He held it carefully aloft for them to see.

"Why is it flat sir?" asked a blonde girl.

"Well we can't be absolutely sure Lauren, because it's been in the ground for a hundred years, but it was found underneath his remains so there's a good chance that he crushed it with his body when he fell,"

"You mean when he was killed?"

"Yes, that's exactly what I mean."

"And he was fifteen?"

"Yes, we believe so."

"But how could he have been there? I thought you had to be eighteen?" asked Josh.

"Strictly speaking nineteen," replied Chris, "but lads were so keen to go they lied about their age and joined up anyway."

"Well why didn't anyone stop them? They must've known they were kids."

Chris nodded, "You'd think so Josh wouldn't you? But times were different. Lads started work at fourteen and sometimes recruiting sergeants were under pressure to sign men up in numbers so they turned a blind eye. Believe it or not some parents even encouraged their boys to go."

There was silence as the group, shoulders hunched against what was now steadily falling snow, gazed at the little grave.

"He had mates just like you; he lived a life, he had parents. Someone is probably living in the house he grew up in, spent Christmas, had birthdays, got into trouble for being cheeky. Maybe someone is sitting in the same classroom where he went to the village school. He was just a boy, a musical boy."

"So how come he's only just been buried?"

"Well Josh," Chris replied," this happens from time to time. The land around here is all farmed for crops so the farmers have to plough it and every so often a plough will turn up some remains or more commonly ordnance."

"Ordnance?" Josh looked confused.

"Anyone?" asked Chris. He'd used the word earlier so he hoped someone had remembered its meaning.

"Bombs and that sir," said a dark-haired girl from somewhere in the depths of her woolly scarf which was wrapped around her face against the now rapidly falling snow.

"That's it, Holly, but more usually shells. It's still very dangerous round here as many of the shells are still live and explode when they're disturbed; every so often we hear of farmers being killed. They call it "The Iron Harvest." He fished in his pocket and brought out a handful of little pointed spent machine gun bullets and dozens of shrapnel balls. "I found all these in a field this morning before I met you. I was only there about twenty minutes and all I had to do was pick up a few handfuls of earth and sift them out so that should give you an idea of just how much is still left in the ground. Unfortunately it's not just this stuff either. There are seventy thousand names on the Thiepval monument of men whose bodies were never found after the Battle of The Somme and the story is much the same in this area as well. Every so often they turn up and the War Graves Commission do their best to identify them from the remains but nine times out of ten it's impossible and they are buried like this lad."

"So what about him then sir, that bugle lad?"

"Well it's interesting because bugles were hardly used on the Front Line, they were mainly for use in camp when soldiers were being trained. Most regiments had their own "call" which might be played on parade and of course the last post was played each evening at the close of the day's activities but obviously they didn't do that in the trenches at the front line; why not? Anyone?"

"It'd tell the Germans where they were sir!"

"Yes it would Josh, but more importantly it might give the impression that they were off duty and vulnerable to attack."

"So why did he have it then?"

"We would only be able to guess, so we will never really know; we can only imagine"

The thin grey light was fading quickly and a pale, yellow sun cast a ghostly light across the faces of the solemn party.

"I know it's cold and it's getting late but I'd like us all to just stand for a minute in silence and think about this young lad and all the others who didn't go home."

A cap of snow was gathering on the top of the little white stone and the fresh green turf was gradually disappearing as the group stood, heads bowed. Usually Josh found these moments difficult and felt guilty because no matter how hard he tried he couldn't stop his mind wandering onto the other thoughts that filled his head but today was different and he found himself wondering about the bugle boy.

CHAPTER THREE:

May 1912

Saturday! Harry couldn't get out of bed fast enough. It was early and the day held adventure . He and his mates were off to Wood End today to try and dam the stream that trickled through the meadow on the edge of Greno' Woods. They'd tried before last summer but hadn't had much success because they were littler and couldn't shift the big stones they needed to do a proper job but this year they'd all grown a bit and Harry reckoned they stood a good chance. He pulled his shirt on quickly and draped the floppy sailor collar over his shoulders, wriggled into his shorts and grunted with frustration as he got entangled with his braces. His boots took an age to button so he left them flopping open as he thundered down the stairs into the kitchen where his mother was already at work washing clothes in a big zinc bath. She stopped as she saw him come into the room, the big copper "posher" still in her hand. She wiped the perspiration from her forehead with a fold of her pinny and pointed at him with a work reddened finger,

"Turn round Harry Jones! Back upstairs and fasten your boots!"

"But mother…."

"No buts my lad, one of these days you are going to come clattering down those stairs and break your neck."

"But.."

She fixed him with a steely blue eye and Harry knew he was beaten; his mother was not someone to argue with. He knew that any attempt would result in the dreaded words, "Your father will have something to say when I tell him you cheeked me!" so he slunk back upstairs, found the buttonhook in the little table drawer and began the laborious task of doing his boots up. Why did they have to be so complicated? Other lads' boots had laces and he was stuck with these stupid old-fashioned things. The sun was beginning to fill the room with a lovely golden light when he'd finished and he took a moment to watch the dust motes dancing in the air before bursting out of his room then taking the stairs back down to the kitchen two at a time which he considered a minor victory as his mum usually told him off for that too.

His mum looked him up and down, smiled and returned to poshing the clothes.

"There's bread on t'table get some toast before you go gallivanting; fire's nice and hot, our Laurie's had his and gone out to play."

Harry cut a big thick slice and speared it with the toasting fork. It was a lovely early summer day but the fire was blazing away to heat the Yorkshire Range and provide hot water for washing. He prodded the bread as close to the flames as he dared and held it there until the kitchen filled with the delicious smell of toast and he could hardly bear the heat on the back of his hand then he spread a thick layer of butter on it, shouted a quick, "Bye!" to his mother and juggling the hot toast from hand to hand to avoid being burnt scooted out of the back door.

He heard his mother shout, "Put t'sneck on!" and he turned and quickly latched the door before setting off to meet his mates. He couldn't understand why his ma would want to be shut inside the furnace of a kitchen on such a warm day but it was a tiny thing like that that could get him in trouble and banned from a day of dam building and he wasn't going to risk that!

He could see the other lads at the corner of his lane and he shouted to them, stuffed the last of the toast into his mouth and broke into a trot. His feet raised a pother of dust as he trotted and he scuffed his boots to raise more so that by the time he reached them he was accompanied by what appeared to be a smoke screen from which he emerged, grinning . The other lads began coughing and spluttering, staggering about and pretending to be on the point of passing out .

"You daft bugger! What you trying to do, smother us?" Frank said through the filter of his jersey which he'd pulled up over his mouth and nose.

Harry laughed, "Laddy-lass! It's just a bit of dust!" and he quickly reached out and whipped Frank's jumper right up over his whole head. Frank began to stumble around, hands outstretched, "Help me! I've gone blind! Blind I tell you !"

"Come on, we've got a stream to dam! We'll never do it at this rate if you silly beggars don't stop mucking about," said Douglas, the tall, gangly lad in a baggy suit of tweeds and a Fair-Isle jersey today. His glasses, mended with a bit of old wire sat lopsided on his serious face. Other more adventurous boys would have used a swear word but Douglas stuck to "beggars." He was a stickler for that sort of thing.

"Well come on then Duggle–arse before you melt! It's going to be hot today and you've come dressed for Christmas!" said Frank and he was off, running down the lane, whipping the heads off the froth of Cow Parsley with a stick, pursued by the rest of the boys. Harry admired Frank and they all considered him their leader but he was also a bit afraid that one day he'd get them into bother as he used "language." He seemed to have no fear and would sometimes cheek grown -ups. Harry always squirmed when he did and was once mortified when a farmer had shouted at them and said he was writing their names down after Frank had told him to bugger off when he caught them in his cow field. Not only that but he'd told the farmer he was called Bobby Sparrow and he lived at twenty three Pigplop Lane which the farmer wrote down laboriously on a piece of paper with a stubby pencil his tongue sticking out of the corner of his mouth. The boys had nearly burst with the effort of keeping their giggles contained but Harry spent nearly a week worrying that his mother and father were going to find out. Today though he just laughed at the rude name Frank had called Douglas; today was going to be grand!

His friend George was waiting on the next corner with a big stone bottle in his hand.

"What's tha got there Georgey boy? Is it ale ? They say thi' dad likes a drop!" Frank said and Harry cringed inside. George's dad was regularly picked up by the Bobbies for being drunk in the street and Harry knew it had a bad effect on George. Harry was proud of his dad; George was ashamed of his.

"They say he once tried to drown a cat under t'pump when he'd had a skinful; scratched him to bits!"

"Gi' oer Frank it's not his fault, just leave him alone will you," Harry said and George gave him a quick smile.

"It's ginger beer, Old Mrs Swift two doors up split her plant and it's just starting to go fizzy. It were reight funny last night, we heard this big bang and a scream and she came running into our back kitchen in her corsets all covered in ginger beer. One of her bottles exploded when she were putting it in't'cellar on t'cold slab. There was a reight palaver and my mam nearly bust a gut laughing at her," George laughed at the recollection, "She were puffing and blowing like a steam train and she used some shocking language but there were a silver lining because we got half her ginger beer plant! She told us it was too lively for her and her heart couldn't stand t'strain! Mind you I don't think I'll ever recover from seeing Mrs Swift in her corsets. It's not summat a growing lad should be subjected to. I might be scarred for life!"

"There's an interesting question here," Frank said seriously, "you've got to wonder what old Mrs Swift was doing going down t cellar in her corsets in t'first place!"

"Come on then," Douglas cut in, "we can talk ginger beer all day but it won't dam a stream," and the lads set off down the lane in the direction of the woods, pushing and jostling and trying to trip each other up.

It was the best day of the summer so far and a blue, cloudless sky met the nodding heads of barley now beginning to ripen in the fields on either side of the lane. Ahead lay Greno' Woods and beyond, Wood End where, running through a wide, lush cow pasture was the little stream they were going to try and block. Poppies were glowing like little hot coals among the corn and somewhere a yellowhammer was shouting it's distinctive call, "A little bit o' bread and no chee-eese." Harry whistled the call back and the little bird suddenly went silent.

"Tha must have insulted it Harry," George said.

"It thinks you're its sweet heart!" laughed Frank and he started singing "I'm only a bird in a gilded cage!" in a stupid girly voice, "I'm appearing at T' Attercliffe Palace next week tha knows,

"Francesca Ramsbottom the wonder of the age! Top of the bill an' all, get a seat in the stalls for a look at my LOVELY legs!"

"Mucky devil!" Harry laughed.

They were at the margin of the woods now, still in bright sunlight in among scrubby little oak trees barely as tall as them and they sought out the steep little path that took them down a slope to where the grand old beech trees marked the start of the ancient woodland. Here, though the trees were widely spaced it was gloomy and cool and Harry gazed upwards at the dense green canopy over his head. There were only small chinks between the leaves where the sky winked and he felt a little rush of pleasure when he remembered his dad's words. "You're looking a history here son. Some of these trees started growing when old Cromwell was in charge! Imagine what they might have seen and they'll be here long after we go an'all."

"What you doing stare bear?"

"Nowt, come on!" Harry gave the lad who'd spoken a playful punch on the arm, got one back and the two friends set off after the others who were trotting through the trees a few yards ahead.

"Wait up then," Sam said "you know I can't run reight fast!" Sam was born with what he described as a "funny foot" which was twisted inwards and dragged a little. He wore a special boot and although he could do everything the other boys could do he had to do it at a slower pace.

"Sorry pal," Harry said, then shouted, "hang on you lot, we're coming!"

The gang paused, looked round and waited until they caught up.

The trees were thinning and ahead the sharp green of Wood End Meadow glimpsed through the gaps made the boys quicken their pace. The cows had been driven away by Frank and Douglas who got there first and were the only two brave enough and the boys were standing by the stream listening to Douglas who had taken charge.

"Right, we need a plan, no good going at this hugger – mugger else we'll end up like last time. We need big sticks and rocks first and we need to find a good spot to dam it an'all. Let's do that first."

The boys began to meander along the bank of the brook until they found a place where there was a wide area where the bank had been trampled down by the cows coming down to drink. The brook ran through the exact centre and was quite deep in the middle. The boys peered into its brown slow moving depths. A whirligig beetle was spinning in the centre encased in its silver sheen of air and tiny freshwater shrimps jerked through the water like clockwork toys.

"This is it, it's perfect , we can make a reight pool here!" George said and there was a murmur of agreement; the beetle would have to take its chances. This was serious work now and a sense of purpose settled over the lads. No one questioned why they were damming the stream, it just had to be done and they were determined to succeed.

"I'm getting rocks for t'bottom, come wi' me Sam my little crippled pal! You might have a funny foot but you're t'strongest lad here."

And although the nasty words stung a bit Sam was so used to hearing them that he just ignored them and concentrated on the compliment about his strength. Frank didn't mean any harm.

The bottom of the brook was soft and muddy and Douglas said that if the rocks were big enough and they threw them high enough they would sink in and form a good foundation for the dam so the boys began foraging for rocks at the field margin. There were the remains of an old building partially buried here so there was a good supply. Suddenly Harry's boot struck something solid and it felt big.

"Hey up lads I've found a belter!"

They'd brought nothing to dig with but soon had sharp sticks broken from the surrounding trees and began scraping around the stone. Within twenty minutes they had prised it loose enough to heft it out of the hole with a great sucking slurp and onto the grass. Harry pulled off his sailor collar and used it to mop the perspiration from his face. It was only nine o'clock but the sun was already hot and he announced proudly that he was, "sweating like a beast!"

The rock was too big to lift and carry so he, George and Sam began to roll it across the meadow in the direction of the stream. It was no easy task and by the time they reached the bank they were exhausted or "knackered" to use the coarse term of which Frank had become fond after he'd heard pitmen using it. He'd tried it out in front of his father and his ear was red for two days after his dad had scutched him one with the flat of his hand and told him that if he ever heard that dirty word coming out of his mouth again he'd really have something to cry about. Today though Frank's father wasn't here; no one's father was here and the lads had all been swearing a fair bit as they grunted and sweated at their work; even Douglas had let a couple go. They felt like men and men swore when they were up against a hard task. It had taken them longer than necessary to dig the rock out because at a crucial moment, just as they were all straining to lever it free from its sticky, muddy tomb the effort had caused Sam to break wind loudly and they had all become weak with laughter and just as they were mastering their giggles Douglas had said solemnly, "Good arse!" without even a glimmer of a smile which had set them off again until they were helpless and shouting "Gi'oer I'm going to wee missen!" as they rolled about on the grass.

"How do we chuck it in?" Sam asked.

"We don't, we roll it, it's heavy enough to sink in on its own,"

"Come on then, let's get it in! Me, Sam and George," Harry said and the three boys found places for their hands and began to heave. It was a good fifty yards to the planned dam and they had to take it in turns to push and roll but after ten minutes they had it balanced beside the stream ready for the final shove. It didn't take much and the rock tipped over the edge of the bank and landed with a satisfying plop in the squelchy mud below.

"Right , we've started, we need another one for the other side then we can build across" said Douglas taking off his suit jacket and rolling his sleeves up. All the boys were in their shirt sleeves now, stockings crumpled round their ankles and boots covered in a mixture of mud and cow muck. Harry had slipped his braces off his shoulders and looking round he thought that apart from the fact that they were all in short trousers they looked like the men at his dad's works. He wished he had a silk scarf like his dad wore to mop the sweat or a big leather apron to keep the muck off his clothes. All the boys knew they were going to catch it when they got home for getting so filthy and depending on how much ale George's dad had

had, he'd probably catch it worse than anyone. But that was later, they'd work to do.

Within an hour the boys had built two higgledy-piggledy little dry stone walls from either bank with a gap in the middle where the stream ran as yet unimpeded and though it was only ten in the morning, Douglas declared it dinner time so they sat in a circle and on a flat stone, pooled their money. There was a beer off shop at the side of the Red Lion pub that sold bread and sometimes boiled ham or cheese and it was only a ten minute walk from Wood End. The boys furkled about in their pockets and the pennies clinked onto the rock. Some lads had more than others but it didn't matter they were all in it together.

Only George looked a bit uncomfortable and Harry knew he had no money, he didn't get pocket spends and things were always tight in his house. Harry put an extra penny in,

"I've got yours Georgie, you gave it me to save when we set off."

He knew he was fooling nobody but all the lads looked relieved that face had been saved. Last to go was Frank and with a flourish he held his hand over the pile and the boys saw a flash of silver as a sixpence fell from his fist.

"Flipping heck! Where'd you get that?" Sam asked. That was six weeks spends in one go.

"Found it!"

"Where, you lucky devil?"

"In me dad's trousers!"

"You pinched it?"

"Let's say a long term borrow,"

"It's nicking that is, you'll get reight done when he twigs on he's a tanner short."

"That's as maybe Samuel but today we feast like kings!"

Frank read books and liked to amuse the boys with fancy talk.

"We can get all sorts of snap with this," Douglas said eagerly and with a last glance at their handiwork they set off. Within half an hour they were back with bread cakes, ham some cheese and an Eccles cake each as well as another pot bottle of lemonade. They were just getting stuck in when Frank suddenly groaned,

"Look what t'cat's dragged in."

The boys followed the direction of his gaze and saw two boys standing at the edge of the wood; Foxy and to their surprise their friend Stanley.

"So that's why he wouldn't come with us when we asked him," Sam said, "got a new mate." Foxy was two years older than most of the gang, including Harry but he liked to have younger lads around him to make him feel powerful.

Foxy trotted towards them,

"Let's have a look what t'kiddies are playing at then," they heard him say to Stanley who was looking increasingly uncomfortable the closer he got.

"It's a highly complicated engineering project Foxy, you'd have to have a brain to understand it," Frank said.

"Thee shut thi gob Frank Ridge or tha'll know about it," Foxy snapped but they could tell by the look in his eyes that he knew he wouldn't stand a chance against all of them so he tried another tack.

"This is private land tha knows and I know t'farmer so I'm going to tell him what you've done in his field, then you'll be for it. He's got a shotgun an'all wi' pepper cartridges and you'll know about it if he shoots you up the arse wi' that !"

"Oh wind your neck in Foxy, we all know tha doesn't know him, you're all talk you, and besides we're making a lovely pool for his cows to drink from," Sam said.

"Tha's got a big mouth for a little cripple," snarled Foxy and he clenched his fist and took a threatening step towards little Sam but Frank and Harry were quicker and they were up on their feet and between them before Foxy's fist could land.

"Gi'oer Foxy," mumbled Stanley and the others gazed at him in astonishment.

"Not reight nice your new pal is he?" Harry said and Stanley pushed his hands deep into his pockets and stared at the ground his face red and a sparkle of tears in his eye.

"Come on lads we've work to do," Douglas said and after a final round of the ginger beer bottle they stood up, letting fly with manly burps and brushing flakes of eccles cake from their shorts.

"Put that lemonade bottle in the stream with a stone on it for later," Douglas called and the work of building began again. For a while Foxy and Stanley just stood watching but the lure was too strong and after a while they too started fetching stones. The technique was to lift them high over-head then drop them into the brook where it ran between the two little walls they had built earlier in the day. Stone after stone was dropped and gradually the gap was blocked and the water began to well into a pool. The water was still gushing through however but Douglas had an idea.

"We want willow twigs now. If we weave 'em in and then stuff leaves and mud in the holes it should work a treat."

It was an easy task and a nice change from humping rocks and the boys soon had a great pile of twigs and branches gathered from the willows that grew along the bank a little further along the stream. Frank and George took their boots and stockings off and slipped into the pooling stream wincing and hooting at the freezing water swirling round their skinny white legs and grimacing as squishy mud oozed up between their toes. The boys began to hand them branches and they were soon busy weaving them into the stone dam under Douglas's direction.

Foxy had other ideas. He'd been on the far side of the brook making sure every stone he cobbed into the water splashed the others. Some had even missed the stream altogether and landed near the other lads. He always shouted sorry but they knew his game and now Stanley was joining in, enjoying the little bit of power associating with Foxy afforded him.

There was a hollow thud and the boys lifted their heads from their work with the branches to see Harry stagger and clutch his head before trying to shout out. No sound came and suddenly his knees buckled and he went down, face first into the pool. Stanley laughed uncertainly then plunged forward, grabbed the back of Harry's shirt and dragged his white face clear of the muddy water.

"Gi'oer messing about Harry," he said then felt many hands shoving him aside as the boys grabbed Harry and hauled him onto the trampled grass around their pool.

"What the chuff did you do that for? You stupid get!" shouted George.

"I didn't mean it, I didn't do it of a purpose!" Stanley said, his voice tremulous and snot beginning to bubble as he began to cry, "It were his idea!" and he looked around but Foxy was a figure in the distance running flat out for the woods.

"He's spark out," said Frank, "give him some air!"

A frightening amount of blood was starting to ooze from a big cut on the top of Harry's head but he was beginning to stir and make funny noises in the back of his throat as the dirty water he'd taken in began to come back up. Douglas quickly reached under his back and turned him on his side and a gush of muddy slush spewed out of him.

Harry's legs began to bicycle then all of a sudden he sat bolt upright with a wild look on his face.

"I can have that done in five minutes!" he shouted, then "Tell him I want four for that price!" Despite themselves a couple of the boys sniggered; it was clear the knock had sent him silly. Harry's eyes were unfocused and his teeth were chattering and blood was now trickling down his deathly white forehead.

"Give him a minute," Frank said. "Mucker Hall was like this when that horse kicked him in t'face last year."

"Mucker" Hall was a local farmer and Frank had been helping him plait his Clydesdale's tail for Whitley Show when it had suddenly taken exception and landed Mucker an almighty kick square in the face with an enormous hoof, spreading his nose almost half way across his face never to return and knocking him silly. He'd talked gibberish just like Harry for fully half an hour after he came round.

"Sit still Harry, tha's had a knock on t'ead and tha blacked out," Sam said as Harry's eyes started to focus again. Harry looked from face to face then said in a small voice, "How come I'm all wet?"

"Because after that rock hit you, you tippled in the stream and we had to drag you out!" Frank said.

"Who chucked it?"

There was an uneasy silence while the boys waited to see if Stanley was man enough to confess.

"It were me Harry," he said after a couple of seconds, "I didn't mean it to hit you, it weren't my idea it were.." But he stopped when he saw the looks on the faces of the other boys. Blaming someone else for what you had done was one of the worst things you could do. British boys took responsibility for their own actions.

"It were me. Sorry," he said simply, "I didn't mean it to hit you I was just trying to splash you."

This was better but only just and he knew it.

"Sorry."

"On the plus side it were Stan that dragged your face clear an'all . You'd have drownded else," Frank said, breaking the horrible tension.

"Come on we need to get you home, can you stand?"

"I think so," Harry said and with the help of Sam and George he stood wobbling on rubbery legs. Blood was running freely now and he wiped his hand across his forehead and looked at it in amazement.

"Bloody hell!"

"Aye I know, you're a reight mess, come on let's get going you might need to have Doctor Frazer look at you," Douglas said and they began the long walk home with Stanley supporting him on one side and Frank the other while the others followed on nudging each other and gawping at the splashes of blood leaving a spotted trail on the path. Apart from encouraging words from time to time they walked in a grim, worried silence. They weren't just worried for Harry either, they were thinking about what would happen when the story came out because they were trespassing after all and maybe Foxy was telling the truth about the farmer and his gun. One thing was certain they were going to get in trouble from their parents with the loss of pocket spends a strong possibility. All in all Saturday was ruined and each of them felt a stirring resentment of Foxy who seemed to have got away scot free yet again.

They had just reached the top of Harry's road, Jonnywham Lane, when a neighbour who was leaning on his gate spotted them. He was a bit of a funny man Mr Leeming and the boys were a bit scared of him because they could never tell if he was kidding them on. He also had an alarmingly large, purple veined nose which it was really difficult not to laugh at so when he called out to them it made the boys jump.

"Nah then! You've been in t'wars young 'un! Let's have a look at you. You can't walk in t' kitchen looking like that , your mam'd pass out! Come on in t'house and let's get you cleaned up."

Harry let himself be led inside and upstairs into a front bedroom where there was a washstand with a jug of water and a mirror.

"Now then, just have a look at yourself before I call Mrs Leeming," said Mr Leeming and he gently manoeuvred Harry in front of the mirror. His face was a completely red mask and his sailor collar and shirt were stained all down the front. Mr Leeming was right, his mother would have passed out if she'd seen him.

"Mrs Leeming! Come and sort this lad out will you he's come a cropper!" shouted Mr Leeming then he winked and said "I know what'll help - drop of brandy, just don't tell your mother!"

Mrs Leeming bustled in as Mr Leeming went off in search of the brandy.

"Let's have a look at you; it's Harry Jones isn't it? I can hardly tell under that lot. My word that is a nasty cut and you've got a proper egg! What happened?"

Harry tried to reply but she was at him with a wet flannel so he had to wait until she'd shifted the blood from around his mouth and nose."

"We were damming t'stream at Wood End and someone chucked a rock and it hit me on my head."

"Someone?"

"Well it were Stanley but it weren't his fault he were egged on."

"By who?"

"I don't like to say."
Even though Foxy was a bully Harry didn't want to dob him in, there was a code among lads that said you didn't tell.

"Well let me see if I can guess. Was it Robert Fox ? He's a bloody menace that kid. Somebody needs to give him a good hiding, give him a taste of his own medicine."

Harry was astounded, he thought he and Sam were the only boys Foxy regularly bullied.

"Here we go young 'un, this'll put hairs on your chest," said Mr Leeming coming in with a little glass of golden brown liquid.

"What's that Ernest?" snapped Mrs Leeming.

"Never you mind my dear it's what the doctor ordered, now swallow it down quick young Harry before Old Mother Hubbard here puts the Kibosh on it!" And he thrust the little glass into Harry's hand. It looked beautiful but it tasted disgusting and it burned like liquid fire as it went down and Harry spluttered and coughed and tears welled in his eyes.

"Told you it were good for you," said Mr Leeming chuckling.

"Fancy giving strong liquor to a bairn," said Mrs Leeming, "you should be ashamed of yourself Ernest Samson Leeming. I'm going to take you to t'Temperance Society and you can take The Pledge."

Tha'll be lucky, old woman, there isn't one round here!"

"Then I'll start one and less of the "old woman" if you don't mind, you silly old fool."

Harry had never heard adults talk like that to each other and he didn't know whether to laugh or be nervous but Mr Leeming kept up a barrage of winks so he guessed it must be all right. He had a warmth suffusing through his chest and though his head was swimmy he did actually feel a little better. A sudden thought struck him.

"Here, are me mates still waiting outside? They can go home, I'll be all right the rest of the way."

"I know, I told them that when I went to get the brandy but they weren't having it. They're all in t'kitchen having a drink,"

Mrs Leeming started in horror , "Oh Lors Ernest you've not given all them lads brandy an' all have you?"

"Don't be daft woman they're having a cup o' watter apiece, they were thirsty after all that work."

Harry was revising his opinion of the Leemings, they were funny and they were kind and nowhere near as scary as he'd always thought. They hadn't once tutted about the fact that the gang were trespassing on a farmer's land or criticised them for building a dam; they just seemed to accept that that's what boys should be doing on a sunny Saturday. He found himself wondering and not for the first time why they had no children of their own.

"Hey up he's here, old Dracula!" said Frank when he walked into the kitchen and though they had no idea what he was talking about the others laughed.

"Tha'd better not blow too hard on that trumpet Harry else your brains'll squirt out of that hole in your head!"

At home that night after old Dr Frazer from up the road had had a look at him and put some white powder that formed a horrible crust on the wound, Harry sat in his dad's old carver chair and told his mother and father and brother Laurie about the day's adventure carefully omitting the bit about Mr Leeming giving him brandy. He endured the telling off that came for dam building on private property though he could tell it was only half hearted and they didn't really mean it and later in bed, snuggled under his eiderdown he chuckled to himself. This would make a grand story to tell the band lads at his next rehearsal. Provided his brains didn't squirt out of the hole in his head when he blew.

CHAPTER FOUR:

June 1912

The Whitsun Marches were to be held on Friday the 7th of June in 1912 and Chapeltown Silver Band were competing for the first time. Harry was hugely excited because this was one of the most important and famous brass band contests in the calendar that attracted thousands of spectators and musicians from all over the north of England and though he knew the junior section had no chance of taking a trophy he couldn't wait to play and hear all the bigger bands doing the same. The contest had been held in the villages of Saddleworth since the end of the last century and one of the reasons Harry was so excited was that the Earl of Wharncliffe had loaned his motorised charabanc to get them across the Pennines. Motor cars were a rarity in the village as most people couldn't afford them so the Earl's huge charabanc, belching smoke and filling the air with its deafening roar was still a great novelty and the idea of actually riding in it was thrilling beyond words. He was on his way to practise and he met euphonium player John Fenwick as he came out of his cottage door.

"Nah then Harry, how's thi noggin? I hear tha's been heading rocks!"

"It's all right ta, I was hoping there might be a scout for Wednesday in t'next field might see my heading skills and sign me up!"

"Aye well don't blow too hard your…."

"Brains might squirt out the hole. I know!" Frank's legendary wit travelled fast. It seemed he was a minor celebrity round these parts. A blood bolted boy staggering home after a vicious rock attack was what passed for high drama in Grenoside even though it wasn't really vicious, just accidental. Nonetheless Harry was looking forward to telling the band lads and was already mulling over a few embellishments as he and John neared the band room. The rock was now twice the size and had been hurled directly at him from ten feet up. He'd lost so much blood Dr Frazer had told him he'd have been dead in an hour if he hadn't reached home when he did and the dangerous and mysterious Mr Leeming had made him drink almost a whole bottle of brandy. The band lads stood round him mouths agape as he grew the story before their very eyes until even he began to believe his own wild hyperbole. Mr Barnes came in in the nick of time as one or two of the older players were beginning to show signs of disbelief . He shouldn't have added that bit about being trampled by the cows as he lay helpless and unconscious underwater.

"Right boys, this is our last rehearsal so let's make it a good one," Mr Barnes said as the lads settled into their seats, "where's Bobby Gregory?"

" He's in t'Infirmary Mr Barnes, his mam said to tell you. Scarlet Fever; they took him in yesterday," said Walter Brennan the band's percussionist.

A murmur ran round the band room. Scarlet fever was the scourge of 1912 in the village and though there was now a pretty good treatment it was occasionally very serious and could kill within days. Some years ago families had lost all their children in one terrible summer and others had been left with damaged hearts after the disease transformed into rheumatic fever.

Although there was sympathy for Bobby there was also fear. Scarlet Fever was spread through coughs and sneezes and here they were cooped up together in a fuggy little room blowing air through instruments and emptying spit out while sitting shoulder to shoulder. It could go through them like wild fire.

"Right boys, rehearsal cancelled we'll have to wing it next Friday. Be outside The Red Lion at two thirty sharp in your walking out uniforms and don't forget your concert uniforms. I've had a word with Mr Roebuck and you're to be allowed out of school at two. Get your mothers to iron them. Harry, you're on sop." Mr Barnes gathered his music, shuffled it into an untidy sheaf which he tucked hastily under his arm, put his cap and jacket on and left as quickly as he'd come.

Soprano cornet or "sop" was the most demanding instrument in any brass band. Until recently the part had been filled by a clarinettist, but now a new instrument pitched in Eb had been developed. You needed a perfect embouchure, power and pinpoint accuracy as well as lungs like bellows to hit the seemingly impossibly high notes. Bobby was two years older than Harry and had worked his way up to the position over the last year and only now was he beginning to show signs of being really up to the job. Harry was stunned and there was silence for a few seconds then John Fenwick began to clap and soon the band room was full of applause.

"Tha can do it Harry, do it for Bobby," one lad shouted.

"There's nobody else good enough, you'll do us proud. Course there'll only be five cornets but we'll blow twice as hard and we can bulk it up wi' t'flugels," said Eric Warren, principal cornet player putting his hand on Harry's shoulder.

"It should be you, Eric, you're principal," Harry said after the applause had died down but Eric shook his head. "I'm only principal because I've been in t' band longer. I couldn't do it like you could, me lip wouldn't last beyond about bar two!"

The brass band world was fiercely competitive and the newly created "sop" chair was the most coveted position so Harry found this generosity of spirit genuinely moving and coupled with that he was terrified! He hadn't even seen the soprano cornet part or even held the instrument so he'd have to go round to Mr Barnes's house, pick up the music and practise like mad if he was going to have any chance of mastering it. He wondered why Mr Barnes had left in such a hurry but that was by the by.

"Well if you're sure," he said, "I'll try my best, I'm not going to let you down if I can help it."

"Tha'll not let us down Harry lad," said John Fenwick, then he turned to the rest of the band, "does anybody know if Bobby's still got his instrument?"

"Aye it's in their parlour, I saw him practising before he got badly," Eric replied.

"Well he can't play that anyway, he might catch t'fever off it," said a tiny lad whose euphonium was nearly as big as him. There was a rumble of agreement and Eric said,

"Are Oughtibridge School Band doing t'Marches this year?"

"No, they're not ready," someone replied.

"Right, they've just got a soprano cornet, I'll ask for a borrow," Eric said, smiling at Harry. "Tha not getting away wi' it Harry me old pork sausage, I can pop over on my bicycle tomorrow afternoon , I'm on mornings so I can get there before they shut and besides I fancy a ride down Jaw Bone Hill!"

Eric loved riding his newly acquired safety bicycle down Jaw Bone Hill between Grenoside and Oughtibridge as it was incredibly steep and fast. Harry's granddad could just remember the Whale's jaw bone which gave the hill its name. It had formed an arch at the peak above Oughtibridge and had been placed there as a route marker for the transportation of whale bone to make corsets in Nottingham. Harry found the story fascinating; the idea of a mighty whale bone ending up on the outskirts of Sheffield seemed outlandish and romantic harking back to a time of adventure and drama on the high seas. The idea of lady's corsets just made him snigger and think of George's neighbour old Mrs Swift and her exploding ginger beer bottle.

"Aye it'll be all right going down but I bet it's a pull coming back up," John said.

"Don't thee worry about me old lad, I'm as fit as a butcher's dog," said Eric with a wink to the lads.

Harry was deeply apprehensive as he left the band room and walked up Wheel Lane towards Mr Barnes' house to pick up the music but he was determined; how hard could it be?

The light was beautiful, dappling through the leaves of the chestnut trees beside the lane and casting a warm glow over the fields that sloped away to the farm buildings of the tiny hamlet of Middleton in the distance. The tiny pea sized conkers were just beginning to form inside their little spiky green jackets and a wren whirred out from among the leaves of the hawthorn hedgerow, churring and chittering at Harry before alighting on a branch, flicking its wings and wagging its stumpy tail in annoyance. Harry paused and watched a shire horse plodding slowly up the hill towards him. He called out to it, "Come on then Captain, come on boy!" and the horse nickered and broke into a lumbering trot. He and Harry were old mates and the farmer had even let him ride on the old horse's broad back the previous winter when he'd been pulling a plough. The bond between old farmer Bemrose and Captain was remarkable; no instructions were needed for the horse to do his job, just a gentle, "Whoa back!" at the end of each furrow and he marked time with his front legs whilst turning on his back legs to start the next row precisely parallel to the last one. Harry loved to watch the shiny earth falling in chocolatey waves slicing away from the silver plough share. Sometimes the earth would give up a little secret like a shard of blue willow pattern pottery or a clay pipe bowl and he was intrigued as to how it had found its way into the middle of a field. Mr Bemrose said it was because people used to have a big heap of rubbish and the contents of their chamber pots at the end of their gardens called a midden and it made excellent fertiliser when it was spread on the land. They used to chuck broken crockery into the mess so bits of it ended up buried. Harry found the idea fascinating and liked to imagine someone dropping a plate on the kitchen flags a hundred years ago or snapping the thin stem of a white clay pipe then trotting down the garden to sling the bits on the stinking heap, grumbling about their bad luck.

Captain nodded his massive whiskery head over the fence and Harry reached out with the flat of his hand for the horse to mumble at the grass he was offering. His muzzle was velvety soft and Harry patted his great flat cheek with his other hand.

"Good lad Captain," he murmured as he swept a length of coarse grey forelock from the horse's kind brown eye.

"Hey up , he talks to horses; good job 'cause he's got no mates!"

The voice made him jump and he turned to see Foxy and Stanley and the rest of Foxy's hangers on watching him from a few yards off .

"I'll get more sense out of him than you talk Foxy," he said and immediately wished he hadn't because though he wasn't scared of Foxy he was petrified of Jim Wragg who was pushing through the other lads in his direction. He was a great brute of a boy who spent more time working on his father's ramshackle farm than attending school and though he was only the same age as Harry he was already the size and bulk of Harry's dad with fists to match and a streak of aggression that made up for his lack of intelligence.

"What did tha' say Jonesy? Does tha' want a smack? Nobody talks to one of my gang like that!"

In the midst of his terror Harry took a tiny bit of comfort when he noticed Foxy looking miffed; he clearly thought he was gang leader not Jim but it was only for an instant because the huge face of Wraggy, red and suffused with fury was bearing down on him. Harry made a quick decision and was over the fence standing at Captain's side before the bully could reach him. He saw the uncertainty in Wraggy's face as he called over his shoulder, "I'm not going in there wi' that Foxy! Its massive."

"What's up Wraggy? I thought you weren't scared of owt!" Harry said calmly leaning against the solid muscle of Captain's shoulder, "I thought you were a farmer's lad."

"I'm not scared of it, I just want to see thee get trampled," he replied, but he didn't move.

"What about you Foxy?" called Harry are you coming in 'ere wi' me and Captain or are you yitten an'all?"

This was a risk as Foxy had grown up around farms too just like Harry and Harry's heart sank as Foxy pushed forward and put his foot on the bottom rung of the fence. Foxy was trying to regain the leadership of his gang but Harry was too quick for him and with the toe of his boot he tapped the great feathered fetlock of the horse and Captain raised a massive hoof and pounded the ground in front of him gouging out a hefty divot of earth that flew behind him, landing with a thud some yards distant. It was a trick Harry had seen Tommy Creaser the farrier use when he was trying to catch a horse's hoof for shoeing and it worked perfectly.

"You're stupid you Jonesy," Foxy shouted, "It'll kill thee that 'oss it's reight dangerous; just tried to stomp on thee!" and he was away shoving his gang before him.

Harry noticed Stan hung back and peeled off towards his own house as Foxy and his mates ran round the corner of Middleton Lane.

Faintly he heard Foxy's voice shouting "He's rubbish at football an' all lads, tried to head a rock!"

"Thanks lad I think you've saved my bacon," Harry said patting Captain's solid, dappled neck. The horse tossed his enormous head twice as if in answer and Harry patted him again, then climbed back over the fence and headed once more for Mr Barnes' house.

Mrs Barnes answered the door which surprised him. He'd only ever seen Mrs Barnes once in the Post Office and he'd almost forgotten she existed.

"Hello Mrs Barnes, I've come for some music off Mr Barnes," Harry said, slightly flustered .

"Who is it Edna?" he heard from somewhere in the house.

"I don't know Norman, says he's come for some music; what's your name lad?" she said .

"Harry Jones, Mrs I've come for the soprano cornet parts for Friday's marches."

"He says his name's Harry Jones, Norman. Says he's a boy soprano and wants his cornet parts or something."

"No Mrs Barnes I want the soprano cornet music please."
"Something about…" she called but Mr Barnes had appeared much to Harry's relief and he was holding a sheaf of music in one hand whilst the other pressed a large handkerchief that smelled of camphor over his mouth and nose .

"Are you all right Mr Barnes?" Harry enquired, slightly puzzled.

"Aye champion Harry but I've a dicky ticker from t'fever when I were a kid and they tell me if I get it again it'll pack in altogether. Is'll be all right in the open air but I'm not risking getting too close to you lads inside just for the present until I can be sure it's passed and nobody's infectious, sorry."

"Oh right," said Harry. So that explained why he'd dashed out of the rehearsal room so quickly.

Harry took the music and headed home through the early evening glow. A great shaft of hazy sunshine was pouring through a gap in the high thin clouds making the buttercups and cowslips in the meadows shine an impossible yellow and the barometer in the parlour of Harry's house had said the fine weather would hold for the next few days. It was going to be difficult finding the discipline to practise after school when his friends would be out playing but he was determined not to let the band down. Today was Monday and Eric had said he would pick the instrument up from Oughtibridge the following afternoon, which gave Harry just two evenings to learn the music and get used to the demands of the soprano cornet. It was a huge mountain to climb and the frustration of waiting was killing him.

"Hey up, you're back early did you forget something?" his dad asked as he opened the door. He was sitting at the table with a newspaper spread in front of him and he whipped his little round reading glasses off as he turned to Harry. Harry filled him in quickly and his dad held out his hand and shook it gravely. This was a rare event as, though his father was a loving, wonderful dad he wasn't a great one for any kind of physical contact now he considered Harry "too old for that sort of thing"

"Tha'll be reight," he said and he ruffled Harry's hair and turned back to his paper.

"Look at this Harry, he said holding the paper out to him. On the front page was a grainy image of a young man in naval uniform and the caption read "James McGrady, steward."

"Another of them poor devils to be buried," Harry's dad said with a sigh, "taken all this time for him to be found."

The sinking of The Titanic in April of that year had caused an unprecedented outpouring of national grief and an uneasy feeling that a solid and reliable England no longer sat quite so comfortably in her Empire. There was a disjoint in the world and though the initial shock and fascination had abated over the last month it was still big news. Harry read the article carefully, James McGrady's poor body had been found floating in the icy waters by a Newfoundland sealing vessel and he was due to be buried that Friday, June 12th in Halifax Nova Scotia. That was the same day as the Whitsun Marches and Harry suddenly felt a twinge of guilt that he was worrying about playing a bit of music in a brass band while thousands of miles away another family was trying to cope with the unbearable grief of losing a loved one in such terrible circumstances. "Should never have happened," his dad grunted, "what a way to go. Do you know they say the band kept on playing as it went down?"

"Aye I'd heard that," Harry said, "played Abide With Me they reckon." If they could do that he could do his job on Friday and do it well; it was nothing compared to that incredibly brave act.

"Why did they play do you think?" he asked.

"I reckon they were trying to keep people calm until the last minute son."

Harry's dad had been badly affected by the tragedy because William Green and Co. for whom he worked had built and supplied one of the great ovens for the ship when she was built and somehow it brought the terrible disaster closer. The men had been so proud that their workmanship would be aboard "The Greatest Ship Ever Built" and now the people who should have feasted on exquisite meals prepared in those ovens were dead, dragged down into the vortex of freezing water as the great liner sank.

"Anyroad up, nowt we can do now. They'll happen find some more in time and then their families can have a bit of peace an'all."
But he was wrong, no more were found after James McGrady, the rest were taken forever by the sea.

CHAPTER FIVE:

June 1912

The sound of chalk scraping and squeaking on slate filled the little school room as the children tried to get to grips with the arithmetic sums Mr Roebuck had written on the blackboard but Harry couldn't concentrate. Two days had passed since Eric, true to his word, had appeared on Harry's back step, red in the face and sweating "Like a dray 'oss" to use his own words.

"I got all t'way to t'top without pushing," he said proudly holding out a little black leather case, "that Jaw Bone Hill's a reight bugg…..," but the swear word was cut short just in time as Harry's mum stepped into the kitchen. "I mean it's very steep. Hello Mrs Jones, me mam says hello an' all, she hopes you're keeping well, lovely weather isn't it?" Eric knew all the worst words and used them freely among his pals but he had been brought up properly and was, as his mother put it, "polite in company"

"Anyway I'll be off, good luck Harry, I'll sithee a' Friday!" and he was off peddling down the lane accompanied by a plume of pale brown dust.

Now it was Friday and Harry had practised until his lip was numb and bruised. The little soprano cornet had frustrated and infuriated him to begin with and he'd "knocked over" note after note until he thought he'd never conquer it but suddenly after a straight three hours of graft the pure sweet notes began to flow and despite the pounding blood in his head and the discomfort of his lip, crushed against his teeth Harry had begun to feel the instrument begin to bend to his will. He played with the cornet muted by stuffing a pair of his woollen stockings into the bell until the early hours of the following morning much to his brother's annoyance and despite the application of arnica cream had suffered agonies the next day when he pushed against the mouth piece and practised again. He was by no means perfect but had found the music quite easy to read and reckoned he could make a decent attempt when the band stepped out.

For now though he had to try and understand some very tricky long division sums. Mr Roebuck was a kindly old teacher and all the boys but one wanted to do well and please him so they were concentrating hard which was more than he was doing. The mid-morning sun had warmed the dusty old room and Mr Roebuck, sitting behind his raised desk and lulled by the gentle scraping of chalk on slate and the murmur of calculation coming from his pupils had dozed quietly off.

A thin drone suddenly entered the room, which turned to an angry buzz as a wasp drifted in, turned and bashed itself against the window behind the teacher's head.

"Hey up, a jasper!" Alfred Simpson whispered loudly and suddenly the morning turned interesting. A wasp in a classroom; a tiny insect floating through the musty air was enough to cause pandemonium among bored boys who needed an excuse to break the tedium.

"It's reight behind old Roebum's head, chuck summat at it afore it stings him,"

"Don't let it near me," said a thin ginger lad sliding out from behind his desk, "I got stung last year on me eyelid and it looked like I'd gone ten rounds wi' him that takes on all comers at t'feast!"

The wasp was on the move and had begun to hover in front of Mr Roebuck's quietly snoozing face. The boys took a sharp intake of breath as it landed on his head and began to crawl about through his sparse hair. One or two sniggered but Cornelius Ridge, known to his pals as Corny was on his feet creeping forward on tiptoe. He had a score to settle as yesterday Mr Roebuck had rapped him over the knuckles with a ruler for not knowing his eight times table and the other lads had laughed and made him feel stupid. He was fourteen years old and was leaving to work down the pit in a few weeks so felt he had nothing to lose. He reached sideways to a tall stack of thick Geography atlases with pasteboard covers which sat on top of a cupboard beside the teacher's desk and carefully picked one up.

"Gi' o'er Corny, tha'll get chucked out," said Douglas in a hoarse stage whisper but he was a lone voice as a teacher with a wasp on his head about to get bashed with a book was about as good as it got on a boring morning in a warm Ecclesfield school room. Corny crept closer, the book grasped firmly in his hand. The wasp continued to explore Mr Roebuck's head with interest occasionally giving a short buzz or stopping to gently clean its antennae with a delicate leg and it clearly tickled the old school master's scalp because he stirred gently and began to raise his hand to brush it away but Corny was too quick and with a great bound he brought the atlas down with a "whump!" on his teacher's head. There was a cacophony of laughter as Mr Roebuck woke with a terrible jerk and a hoarse cry of surprise, banging his knees violently under the desk and clutching his head as he stared round the class with wild eyes.

"What the blazes!" He shouted, "Which boy did that? What the devil do you think you're doing you blethering jackasses!"

But there was more fun to be had because the wasp, which had been enjoying itself on Mr Roebuck's head, had been missed and was now angry and as Corny tried to evade Mr Roebuck's flailing grasp it settled on the end of his nose and sank its sting deep into the tip. Corny howled and swept it away with his hand, tears starting from his eyes.

"Not so tough now are you Ridge?" said Mr Roebuck, "and I'm going to make something else sting now! Get over here lad, I'm going to give you a thrashing you'll never forget!" and he opened the cupboard beside his desk and took out a long whippy cane. The boys all knew this horrible instrument as "The Stinger" and it was clear Corny was in for it as Mr Roebuck's head was bright red; a sure and rare sign of his anger.

"Hey up Corny, thi arse'll be as red as thi nose in a minute," a lad shouted but he soon shut up because the infuriated wasp was buzzing around his head. Pandemonium broke out with boys standing on their desks and others veering around the room swatting at the increasingly furious wasp with their slates.

"Sit down you foolish boys, If any boy breaks their slate then his father will pay for a new one!" shouted the teacher, one hand grasping Corny by the collar of his jacket, the other wielding "The Stinger" as he tried to bend the lad over for his punishment. Corny was crying now as the pain of the wasp sting was excruciating and though he wasn't afraid of The Stinger he was feeling humiliated.

"Tha'll not cane me Roebuck," he blubbered and he squirmed out of the master's grip and, turning a desk over as he went, ran for the door.

"Stop that boy!" Mr Roebuck shouted but it was in vain, Corny was gone, wailing and clutching his nose leaving the door wide open through which the wasp and a torrent of shouting, hooting boys followed him .School was over for the day and old Mr Roebuck didn't have the energy to chase them. He put The Stinger back in the cupboard and sat down heavily, wondering what the younger generation was coming to.

The boys all knew that they'd be in big trouble tomorrow but for now they were free on a glorious June day.

"Come on Harry, let's go and finish our dam," said Sam cheerfully, "we can get it done if we all pitch in."

"Can't Sam, I'm playing this aft so I'm going to practise for an hour."

Sam gaped at him uncomprehendingly then with a shrug said, "Suit yourself, we're all going." And trotted off with his funny shambling gait to where the others had gathered under the huge chestnut tree outside Creaser's blacksmith's forge. Tommy Creaser and his deaf and dumb brother Frank who worked alongside him stood amongst them drinking tea from giant tin mugs and waved them off before turning and going back into the dingy forge where after a short while the sound of Tommy's great hammer started to ring on the anvil again, the bell-like sound clear and sharp in the shimmering air of the hot afternoon.

Harry watched them go and felt a huge pang of jealous regret but a band job was a band job and you had to be "match fit" especially playing a new and unfamiliar instrument.

CHAPTER SIX:

June 1912

At two twenty Harry was outside The Red Lion pub wearing his hot, itchy walking out uniform and with his concert uniform wrapped in brown paper tucked under his arm. It was made of heavy serge and was black with gold trim and he knew he would feel even more hot and uncomfortable if the sun continued to beam down. Most of the rest of the band had gathered now and some of the older lads were smoking and laughing together a little way off. These boys had left school and considered themselves men though they were still in their teens. The Whit marches were seen by many in the Brass Band world as a great excuse to drink themselves silly after they had competed and some of these lads who looked a little older were planning to join in.

"I'm havin' a reight skinful me!" bragged Bartholomew Baxter, "I'm used to it any way, I've had eight pints before now." The truth was he'd once had three and was as sick as a dog behind his nan's shed but the other lads were in no mood to challenge him as they were too busy boasting about their own drinking prowess. Harry and the younger lads sought out some shade in the lee of the pub wall where a few of them were playing "Knucklebones" watched by the rest. John Fenwick was next to go and he was well known to be "hot" at the game. He took the five little knobbled bones or "jacks" in his right hand and tossed them in the air. He quickly turned his hand over and caught all but one on the back of his hand. He could get as far as "foursies" which would put him in the lead over Eric who'd only managed "twosies".

"Give me the ball then," he said and a lad solemnly handed him a heavy red india rubber ball. He knelt and spread the jacks evenly on the ground in front of him then bounced the ball hard beside him. His hand was a blur as he snatched the little bones up, grabbing the last one as the ball landed with a thud beside him.

"Foursies! And that my friends is how to play knuckle bones!" he said with a grin of satisfaction.

A great roar cut short his crowing as The Earl of Wharncliffe's horseless charabanc rounded the corner in a huge cloud of dust. It was driven by old Billy Spratt, the Earl's coach driver, who'd not made the transition from driving horses to driving this huge terrifying monster easily. To the band lads it was a wonder and they all cheered as it approached; Billy gripping the steering wheel with white knuckles, his face transformed into a rictus of terror as he wrestled the machine to a throbbing, clattering standstill in front of the ale house.

"Tha'd better all get in," he shouted, wiping his brow and straightening his hat, "I've got to get thee ovver t'flamin' Pennines in this. I doubt we'll live so if tha wants to settle on some last words for your families now'd be a good time," he added with a ghoulish gap toothed grin.

The lads scrambled for the heavy back doors and clambered aboard pushing and jostling for outside spots on the wooden bench seats. The body of the charabanc was like a long boat and there were eight benches running across from side to side with a narrow walkway down the centre. The best place was on the outer seats where you could rest your arm on the side instead of being squashed in the middle where there was constant elbowing for room and you were thrown from side to side as your bottom slid about on the polished wood. Harry was right in the middle as the older lads had claimed all the best places.

"Reight! Hold onto yer 'ats, we're off!" Billy shouted as he clambered into the cab. He pressed the accelerator to the floor so the engine roared, released the clutch and brake at the same time and in a cloud of stinking black fumes the great beast leapt forwards only to stall immediately, throwing the band off balance so they yelled and swore as they bashed into the backs of the lads in front.

"Bloody hell Billy, go steady I nearly smacked me mouth on the back of Tom's head ; I'd be a reight player wi' no teeth!" shouted Ernie Slynn who played euphonium, "and any road where's Mister Barnes? He isn't on here tha knows!"

"I've to pick him up at his house so let's try again," said Billy hopping down from the cab and feeling about under the running board for the starting handle.

He inserted it in its socket at the front of the engine and gave it an almighty heave but the engine turned once, backfired and nearly

jerked his arm out of its socket as the compression spun the handle violently into reverse. Billy swore and said,
"You knew where you were with hosses, give 'em a touch of the whip and they go forrards, pull on t'reins and they stop," he grumbled, "This bugger does what it wants, it nearly broke me arm then!"

After a great deal of sweating and cursing eventually the engine burst into coughing, clattering life and after picking up a nervous looking Mr Barnes from his home they were off. The speed was breath-taking for lads who had only ever travelled in hay carts and other horse drawn vehicles and they were giddy with excitement and terrified at the same time as the ungainly machine bounced and careered along the rutted roads heading towards The Woodhead Pass through the lowering Pennine hills. Most of the band had never been much further than their villages except for the occasional trip into Sheffield so the great hills purpled over with flowering heather and riven by sparkling streams plunging down narrow gullies were an awe-inspiring wonder to them, so different to the gentle woods and fields they were used to.

"I might get on t'train and come out here one weekend, we could have some grand adventures scrambling up them rocks," someone said and there was a rumble of agreement as the boys gazed at the towering gritstone crags they were passing beneath.

"Tha'd like as not get shot," shouted Billy from the driving seat, "tha can't just wander about out here tha knows, it belongs to t'gentry so they can come with their rich pals and shoot little birds when they feel like it. It's not for the likes of us hoi polloi, we're only allowed to look from a distance."

After an hour Billy pulled the "Chara" over and the band clambered down to the roadside groaning and stretching and rubbing their aching backsides. A little of the shine had worn off their initial excitement because it had become fiendishly uncomfortable and the jerking and bouncing had made some of them feel somewhat queasy.

"Tha's got ten minutes for a bit o'snap and if any of you ladies need a piddle now's your chance," grunted Billy, "Don't wander off or I'll leave you behind and there's wolves and bears and all sorts of things that'll eat little lost boys on these moors tha knows."

"Aye and there's savage sheep that kill daft old drivers an' all," said Eric.

Most of the boys had brought bread and cheese wrapped in greaseproof paper and barring one or two whose green hue and quiet demeanour told of their sickly stomachs they gobbled it down knowing their next chance to eat would be after they'd marched. A good number of them had aching bladders and they took the opportunity to relieve themselves after they'd eaten.

"Oy ! face t'other way you mucky devils," Billy shouted, "You've hundreds of miles of moorland to piddle on and you do it against t'bloody wheels!"

The rest of the journey passed almost without incident except for a close call with a sheep that wandered onto the narrow winding road in front of the charabanc causing Billy Spratt to swerve violently and shout a word even the most grown up lads had rarely heard and certainly never used.

Saddleworth was a grim, foreboding place of mills and factories for the rest of the year but today the villages were a tapestry of colour with bunting strung across the main streets and the huge banners of the brass bands being proudly displayed. Harry's band was to march up Dukinfield Main Street along with all the other junior section bands. They would be marked twice, once for deportment, or their ability to march perfectly in time and again "blind" by a team of adjudicators who sat hidden in a little dark green canvas tent for the entirety of Friday afternoon and evening until all the bands had marched past them. They didn't know the order of the bands so they couldn't be biased which was important as they all either played or conducted in their own bands. Caesar Baxter who was a slightly odd lad who played the trombone had a burning question troubling him. He tapped Mr Barnes on the shoulder,

"Mester Barnes? You know how the adjudicators stay in that tent for all them hours?"

"Yes Caesar," Mr Barnes replied. He was busy reading his score and could do without the boy prattling in his ear, "what is it? I'm busy so this had better be important."

"Well, I was wondering!"

"What lad? Come on spit it out, I've got a lot to do."

"Well, where do they …… you know!"

"A bucket lad, now any more daft questions or can I get on?"

Harry thought that took the mystique of the god like judges down a peg or two and he made his mind up there and then that adjudicating wasn't for him.

A grim looking man with a massive bushy moustache and wearing a bowler hat and a frock coat was making his way from band to band giving each conductor a slip of paper. "Here we go, it's the draw lads," said Mr Barnes . He was hoping for a middle place as first and last bands rarely won .

"Now then Eric," he said to the man, "what's tha got for us?"

The man handed him a slip of paper with great solemnity and said, "Position four Norman, a grand draw."

"How many in this section?"

"Eleven." The two men shook hands and Eric Ollerenshaw moved on to the next waiting group of young musicians.

"Mr Barnes looks chuffed," John Fenwick remarked, "Four's a grand draw, provided we don't muck up we're in with a chance of a place at least."

"We've half an hour before proceedings get under way so follow me lads we've time for a quick run through," Mr Barnes shouted and the band traipsed after him to a patch of rough ground behind The Angel Inn on King street. It was the strangest rehearsal they'd ever had. The piece was written by J Ord Hume and was titled "The Elephant" as he'd been staying at the famous Elephant and Castle Inn in London when he composed it. The difficulty was marching and playing at the same time whilst reading the music that was clamped to their instruments. They kept stumbling and treading on each other's heels as they couldn't see much ahead of them and a small crowd had gathered to watch and were chuckling at their seeming ineptitude but Mr Barnes ignored them and kept the boys at it, "Stomp like elephants! Crowd'll like that!" he shouted.

Bart Baxter looked put out and mumbled "Bloody stupid this, we look a reight set o' Charlies," and when Mr Barnes wasn't looking he whipped into the side door of the pub and left them to it. Walter Brennan ventured a question, "What if t'crowd don't know the name of what we're playing though Mr Barnes, they'll think we've gone doolally tap!"

"Don't you worry Walter lad, these folks come every year, they know their music."

So it was that in the mid afternoon sun a stranger passing by would have seen a gaggle of young musicians stomping hard round a field with an elderly man waving his arms and shouting "Like elephants boys! Like elephants!"

Eventually after what seemed like an age it all started to come together and the boys began to enjoy their odd rehearsal.

"Now remember lads once you're marching you're on your own so play up and for heaven's sake keep in time. Now …" but he got no further because there was a sudden commotion at the pub door as a big man in a collarless striped shirt and long calico apron emerged dragging a struggling Bartholomew Baxter by his collar and trouser seat. He slung him unceremoniously onto the tussocky grass and growled, "And stay out!" Then he turned towards Mr Barnes, "One o' yours is he?" Mr Barnes had to admit he was. "Aye well he's had two pints chalked on t'slate and when it comes to, he hasn't a brass farthing to settle up and I've a suspicion he isn't of age either. Now cough up or this is going to t'pawn shop !" He reached back into the pub doorway and swung Bart's euphonium case into view. With a sigh Mr Barnes said, "How much landlord?"

"A tanner, that's threepence for the ale and threepence to compensate for all t'custom I lost when he started parping on that flaming thing and half my regulars walked out!"

Mr Barnes fumbled two little silver coins into the man's hand, apologised for the inconvenience and turned to Bart who was sitting on the grass looking decidedly out of sorts.

"Well Bartholomew Baxter, you've made a proper exhibition of yourself haven't you lad? Your father will have to hear of this I'm afraid."

"Oh don't Mester Barnes, I'm sorry I won't let you down again I'm really…" but he stopped, went very pale and glassy eyed and was suddenly, gloriously sick on the grass. The band lads all cheered and Bart wiped his mouth with the back of his hand, staggered unsteadily to his feet, gave them all a wan smile and said weakly, "Better now, I'm reight sorry everybody, I've let you down." To everyone's astonishment big tears welled in his eyes and spilled down his still greenish cheeks. Mr Barnes broke the spell of embarrassment which had struck all the boys dumb, "All right let's put all this nonsense behind us, we've a job to do, everybody back to the charabanc, it's time to get your concert uniforms on." There was a mumble of relief from all the lads and John Fenwick who had a strong streak of kindness put his arm round Bart's shoulder and said, "We all make mistakes Bartholomew, put it out of your mind, we can't do this without you, you know. You're a grand Euph player now pull yourself together and nowt more'll be said. Just play your heart out and even old Norman'll forgive you. I'll tell you what though there'd better be no more talk of supping eight pints if that's what happens when you have two."

The brass band only worked because all the boys and young men depended on each other's loyalty and commitment with every component vital and working together to make the big musical machine run in perfect harmony.

The heavy leather roof of the chara had to be wrestled into position to afford a bit of privacy for the lads to change and Harry was one of the last out after they had all scrambled into their uniforms. He made a vow to himself then and there that he would ask his parents for laced boots for his birthday in August. The buttons had taken forever again and the other lads got impatient. "Come on Jonesy, we're competing this year tha knows!" It was all right for the first and second section bands, they were allowed to change in the back rooms of pubs but Harry's band were all too young despite Bart Baxter's attempt to show he was a man.

Heavy, dark clouds had begun to gather by the time Chapeltown Silver Band were standing at the starting line for their march and the change in temperature had knocked some of the tuning of the delicate brass instruments out but they were soon back in as Mr Barnes had the uncanny ability to pick out minute variations even among the cacophony of more than twenty instruments trying to retune at the same time.

Eric Ollerenshaw held his big silver pocket watch and watched the steady seconds tick past until the hand reached the twelve then he brought his raised hand down, blew a whistle and they were off.

The performance went by in a blur for Harry. He was dimly aware of spectators lining the route, waving little paper flags and he clocked the deportment adjudicators as they passed them seated stiffly on a bench beside the road but other than that he was concentrating so hard on playing the tricky, unfamiliar little instrument, keeping in time as he marched and reading the music that he was astounded when they made a second pass of the adjudicators and stood in front of the "blind" adjudication tent in band formation to play their second test piece "The Black Knight." This was an easier task as the band stood still but that meant the quality of the playing had to be absolutely perfect. Harry held his own and was proud that he didn't knock a single note over. With a massive crescendo the rousing musical march came to an end. A sound took Harry by surprise and it was a couple of seconds before he realised that it was applause from the crowd in the little square where the march finished. He lowered his instrument and took in the scene; he was going to remember this moment for the rest of his life. Hundreds of smiling faces were looking towards the band and a blur of hands rang out a great peal of applause. It was a wonderful scene, the men in their best clothes and even the occasional top hat or straw boater and the women in pretty spring dresses of pastel shades. Most of them were wearing wide brimmed hats decorated with spring flowers and many were twirling little fringed parasols. Harry thought he had never seen anything so colourful and he was filled with a surge of emotion that he couldn't quite pin down but which was something to do with the way a late Spring day makes anyone feel; full of anticipation and impatience for the coming warm days and the swelling of the year.

"Not bad lads," said Mr Barnes and the band lads grinned with pride. "Not bad" was very high praise from their conductor.

The next band were lining up and there would be no news for several hours so the Chapeltown Junior Silver Band were dismissed with a severe warning to stay out of mischief and be back outside the Angel Inn at six o'clock to hear the Junior section results.

"Outside Bartholomew, not inside, understood?" Said Mr Barnes and with a whoop of excitement the lads were off. It was a day of colour and music and treats. There was a magnificent carousel set up at the top of the village and for a penny a go you could make yourself feel happily dizzy whizzing round astride a brightly painted horse or even a tiger or unicorn. From the main street the sound of the first and second section bands rang through the village at regular intervals and Harry snuck away from his mates a couple of times to listen to them. Competition here among the most accomplished adult bands was fierce and the men who had drawn at the latter end of the day were stone cold sober whilst those who had already played were thronging the pubs and standing in the streets with tankards and glasses of beer in their hands shouting and joshing with each other now the pressure was off.

Harry, clutching a brown bag of sticky cinder toffee, was listening to Brighouse Band full of wonder at the sheer power of the adult players. They had yet to get a soprano cornet and Harry could see the conductor desperately signalling to the band to soften their sound in quieter passages so the thin reed notes of the clarinet could cut through but he was having little success and the poor clarinet player's face was puce with effort as he blew with all his might. The instrument's days were numbered and Harry permitted himself a little smile; at least he'd been heard.

"Here we go then ," muttered Ernie Slynn once the junior section bands had gathered in the pub yard to hear the results. Harry prepared himself to be disappointed but still his finger ends tingled with nervous anticipation as Mr Ollerenshaw stepped onto a little wooden platform which had been heaved into place by the pub landlord and his cellar man. A hush descended as the team of six adjudicators in black suits and bowler hats joined him. Their faces gave nothing away and they studiously avoided making direct eye contact with the crowd of band lads in front of them.

"I'd like to introduce you to mester 'arold Batty who is chair of the hadjudicators who would like to say a few words to you boys."

One of the assembled men stepped forward and after a degree of harumphing and throat clearing, began to speak.

"Now then lads, it's been a grand day and we've heard some excellent music but not everybody can win so some of you will 'ave to go 'ome disappointed but you've heard the section bands playing today and those men got there because they didn't give up, they kept playing and improving. In a few years time some of you will be playing with them and maybe in the future one or two of you might even be adjudicatin' like me and my colleagues 'ere."

He was a puffed up little fat man who looked as though he might explode out of his tight checked waistcoat at any minute. He had an enormous walrus moustache and his bowler hat perched precariously on the top of his head. Harry thought being in that little green tent with him must have been a very tight squeeze and he didn't even let himself imagine the horror of the bucket arrangement. He nearly got the giggles but he stifled them in time to hear Mr Ollerenshaw say,

"Thank you Mester Batty for those wise words now if you would be so kind as to 'and me the marks?"

With great solemnity the adjudicators handed him their mark sheets and after a good deal of shuffling and close examination Mr Ollerenshaw began to speak.

"Remember boys three hadjudicators 'ave marked you blind so they 'ave no hidea what the name of the bands was when they marked you, just your marching order which I kept 'idden from them," His attempt to speak "properly" in front of the adjudicators tickled the lads but this was too tense a moment for laughter.

"The other hadjudicators 'ave marked you for deportment and both scores 'ave been hadded together. I now 'ave your results so listen carefully."

The list crept upwards from eleventh place for a brand new band of very young lads and the boys in Harry's band held their breath as band after band were named below them.

"In Fourth place , Barnsley junior band,"

So they were placed ! At least a place. Harry's heart swelled with pride as he heard Mr Ollerenshaw say, "Third spot goes to Chapeltown Silver Juniors. Well done lads! Somebody step up 'ere and get your cerstificate."

"Go on Eric," John Fenwick shouted and Eric Warren stepped reluctantly forward. With ears bright red with embarrassment Eric shook the hands of the adjudicators and finally Mr Ollerenshaw and was handed a scrolled certificate with a purple ribbon round it. Eric held it aloft to rousing cheers then scuttled back down to his bandmates who crowded round to look at it.

"It'll look grand in a frame on the band-room wall," said Norman Barnes proudly.

The return journey was if possible even more exciting than the ride to Saddleworth as Billy Spratt told them he had enjoyed his day and was in a state of "advanced refreshment" to use his own phrase. Mr Barnes was reluctant to let him drive but Billy assured him that he was no more likely to kill them all drunk than he had been sober and unless they met another chara coming the other way they were safe in his hands which the boys noticed were shaking visibly.

"Tha'll be all reight wi' me Norman lad, I drive better when I've 'ad a few. We'll be home in record time," he said before attempting to turn the starting handle. Incredibly he managed it first time and after the leather cover had been closed against the heavy spots of rain which were beginning to fall they were off. It was cosy inside the dark interior of the charabanc and though they were thrown about alarmingly as Billy threw the machine recklessly round corners the boys enjoyed their death defying ride home. The glow of victory was about them and they sang lustily as the great beast roared through the lashing rain and into the Pennine night. Thankfully no other vehicles were encountered and barring a stop for Billy to relieve himself against the wheel of the chara they made good time and were back outside Mr Barnes' house by eleven pm.

"Tha looks a tad pale Norman," grinned Billy as he clambered down, " 'ave I freetened thi?"

"No, no Billy, just not used to it that's all."

"Come 'ere Norm," Billy beckoned him with a crook of his finger and when Mr Barnes leaned close he breathed heavily in his face.

"Can tha smell owt?"

Mr Barnes reeled from the smell but it wasn't beer on Billy's breath, it was onions. "Cheese and onion sarnie for me dinner, tha didn't reckon I'd risk these lads' lives did tha Norm? I were havin' em on, make it seem a bit more excitin' like. I haven't touched a drop since t'day afore yesterday now get thissen home, t'landlord o' t'Red Lion said I could leave this bugger in his coach house and have a pint with him if I got you all back in one piece before midnight. It turns back into a turnip come the stroke of twelve."

"Tha means a pumpkin!" shouted one of the younger lads who'd seen Cinderella at The Sheffield Empire the winter before.

"Not this bugger, it'll never be owt but a turnip in my book,"

Harry's dad and brother Laurie were in the kitchen when he arrived home with a pot of tea between them on the table.

"He's here!" Harry's dad said rising and stepping towards him to ruffle his hair.

"Go on then, how did you do?" Laurie asked.

"Oh, not bad: third," he said trying to assume a nonchalant voice.

"Out of how many?"

"Eleven"

"Not bad lad," his dad said.

"Not bad ? NOT BAD?" Laurie said, "It's a bit more than that, it's blooming champion!"

"Aye I know," his father smiled, "but we can't have his head swelling up now can we? He'll not be able to get through that door. Cup of tea our Harry then bed, you can tell us all about it in t'morning."

"Where's mam?" Harry asked

"Went to bed half an hour back, she fell asleep in t'rocking chair, she were worn to a frazzle. She's doing too much again and I keep telling her but she won't slow down."

Sitting in that warm kitchen with his father and brother drinking tea while the rain pattered against the window would be a memory Harry would return to again and again. He didn't think he'd ever be this happy again

CHAPTER SEVEN:

June 1912

Saturday broke bright again and Harry was up and out by eight in the morning. He was on his way to his friend George's house. Harry had already told his family all about the competition and though he was as pleased as punch he didn't brag or crow, just told them the facts and made them laugh with tales of Billy's driving. His mother was so proud he'd had to suppress a wobbly lip and look the other way when she reached out and hugged him to her.

"Our Harry, the famous trumpet player! Just imagine," she said.

"Cornet mam! And hardly famous, we came third," he protested but inside he was bursting and he couldn't wait to tell George. He was the only one of his mates who showed any real interest. The rest just wanted him to "do a turn" every so often. George lived in "The Lanes" a notoriously rough part of the village where a dozen or so tiny, crumbling cottages were crowded on top of each other along either side of a dank, overgrown gully where the sun seldom penetrated. Elder bushes and deep green ivy grew in profusion and the tiny dwellings seemed slumped in despair. Their front gardens were rank with nettle and dock and if George hadn't been his best friend Harry wouldn't have ventured there because it frightened most children. But he was a fiercely loyal lad and he and George had been inseparable for their whole lives. George's house was damp and smelled terribly of the black mildew that grew on the walls. Rags hung at the windows instead of curtains and there was scarcely any furniture. Just a plain deal table and a few rickety hard backed chairs in the kitchen. Harry had only been upstairs once and was horrified because there were no beds and George and his little sister slept on a heap of filthy blankets in the corner of the same room as their father who had a thin mattress on the floor covered in blue and white ticking with a heap of old coats for covers. There was another room but George went very quiet when Harry mentioned it and mumbled something about it being locked "because of what happened to Ma." Harry didn't ask again. Sometimes you just didn't.

"Going to visit thi little pal in his hovel? If tha gets there afore nine his father might still be sober."

Foxy stepped out from the alley beside the Stocks pub where he'd been smoking one of his father's cigarettes stolen when his back was turned that morning.

"Shut thi mouth Foxy, it isn't his fault."

Harry knew that George's father had taken to the bottle after George's mother had died giving birth to a little girl who also didn't survive. The grief of both losses had almost destroyed him and now, though he managed to get farm labouring work to earn enough to feed himself and George and George's sister Sarah, any extra money went on drink. Harry understood and he felt oddly guilty that his own family was so perfect compared to the lot that his best pal had been dealt.

"Mek me, you puny little laddy lass," sneered the older lad taking a menacing step towards Harry. "I'll paste thee if tha says that again'"

"Oh aye? You and whose army?" Harry realised he'd gone too far and before he could make a break for it Foxy had darted at him and grabbed the front of his shirt. The first blow winded him and dropped him to his knees and the second made his ears ring . He struggled but Foxy was too strong and he felt himself being violently rolled over onto his back and then Foxy's bony knees pinioned his arms and hard fists were pounding his face making tears start in his eyes and blood trickle from his nose. Just as he thought he was going to pass out Foxy suddenly lifted off him, a startled panicky expression on his face, seemingly floating upwards into the air.

"Leave him alone you little sod, he's half your size," came a voice from behind Foxy's struggling silhouette.

"Are you all reight lad? Get up if tha can, I've got him, he can't hurt thi."

Foxy's voice was high pitched and mewling as he dangled by the collar from George's dad's big hand.

"Get off me, I'll get thee done, me dad'll get thee when I tell him."

"No he won't because from what I've heard he's as big a bully as thee Robert Fox, and bullies only pick on people smaller than them because they're cowards, now get away before I give thi summat to really whine about."

With a final shake like a terrier shaking a rat George's father set the struggling, blubbering lad down and released him. There was a big, tell-tale wet patch on the front of Foxy's trousers.

"Not very clever now are you son? Run home and get your old man to give you a bath before the smell of that gets too bad."

Foxy ran, stumbled, fell, picked himself up and ran again turning and shouting unintelligible threats and insults once he was far enough away to be safe.

"Ignore him Harry. Are you all right lad? He'd got you down in a patch of nettles, you must be stung to bits." He scouted around and handed Harry a big, cool dock leaf. "Rub your legs with this, it'll settle the sting down."

Harry hadn't noticed the nettle stings because his nose was throbbing and one of his eyes was beginning to close but now he realised his legs were smarting like a hundred crawling ant bites and he rubbed the big leathery dock leaf vigorously up and down his calves.

"Thanks Mr Fletcher, I'm all right now." Harry lied, "He's always after me for something, I wish he'd just leave me alone."

"Aye well happen he'll think twice now he's had me to deal with. Bullies like him are always cowards, his dad was the same when he was a lad, I went to school with him and he was always chucking his weight about. Like father like son eh?" He looked Harry up and down and with a nod as if to say, "You'll be alright," then turned to go back into his house. "I'll get our George for you. Keep away from Robert Fox, he's no good."

"Aye, well I know that!" thought Harry touching his bruised cheek carefully. He was due a proper shiner of a black eye and was wondering how he would explain it away at home when George appeared at the cottage door.

"Me dad told me what happened, he'd better stop now or all t'village'll find out he wet hissen ," he said, "come on let's go and see if anybody's out, I heard Frank's got a new casey we might be able to get enough together for a game of togger. Football wasn't Harry's passion and the heavy leather "casey" ball was a terrible thing when it smacked you hard on a bare thigh but the kind of football he and his pals played in a local cow field was a hilarious affair that wasn't taken at all seriously. Games sometimes lasted all day on and off and once word got round, as many as thirty kids of all ages would arrive including one tough, black haired girl who could out run, out tackle and out dribble most of the boys on the field.

They set off back towards the field that served as their pitch chattering about Harry's day in Saddleworth. He told George all about the episode with Bartholomew and went cold with embarrassment when George said matter of factly, "He wants to meet up with my pa, that'd make him think twice about drinking ale."

"Sorry George, I didn't mean owt, telling you that."

"It's all right Harry, I know what he's like."

Harry thought hard and couldn't put the two versions of George's father together. There was the big gentle man with soft, tired eyes who had rescued him from Foxy and the man who came roaring in at night and took all his anger at an unfair world out on his children. It didn't fit.

"Hungry?" Harry asked.

"No, I'm all right he bought some bread yesterday and t'chickens had laid this morning so I've had some scramble on toast, it were lovely. Made some for our Sarah an' all."

Frank joined them carrying a dark brown leather casey ball.

"That's a blinder, where did you get it from?" George asked

"Present," Frank said with a wink but both Harry and he had spotted the letters WRCC stamped in black ink underneath the ball's lacing.

"A present from West Riding County Council, a very generous organisation, outstanding chaps to a man," Frank said. He'd nicked it from school.

"You're a reight wrong 'un Frank Ridge they'll hang you before you're twenty," George laughed. Old Mr Watson who was in charge of the big store cupboard where hoops and balls and bean bags were kept was a terrible hoarder and half the stuff in there had never been touched. Frank had just "liberated" the ball for its proper use.

"Hey up there's Stanley," Harry said as he spotted a figure sitting on the fence of the cow field.

"Nah then Stan, where's thi new mate?"

"No pal of mine, tha can't trust him as far as tha can chuck him. He had a bob off me last week and he says he never had it so I'm a bob down and he's been eating spice every day for a week."

"Why did you give it him then?" George asked.

"Not like I had a choice is it? He said he'd smack me if I didn't cough up."

George was about to tell him what his dad had done to help Harry but he thought better of it because he didn't want Stanley to think Harry couldn't stick up for himself. "Come on let's have a kick about, forget about him," he said and the four lads scaled the fence into the field.

"Three and in?" suggested Harry, "I'll go in first."

George and Stanley tugged their pullovers off and made a goal mouth and Harry threw the ball out into the bumpy field of long grass, buttercups and thistles. "Not exactly Owlerton Stadium is it?" Frank shouted as the ball bobbled and bounced in all directions.

"No its better! Now Bramall Lane that's a proper ground," yelled George. It was fun having two teams in the city and though none of the boys had ever attended a single match they were firmly allied to either Sheffield Wednesday or Sheffield United.

"Get away with you, Bramall Lane's a cricket ground where they try to play a bit of football ."

"Aye well I've heard Wednesday are that rubbish at football they tried to get people to come and see a Cowboys and Indians show at Owlerton instead!"

Frank had the ball and was dribbling round Stan's feet using all manner of fancy footwork most of which was wasted as the ball kept bouncing off divots of tussocky grass and scooting off in unexpected directions.

"Ah well that, Georgina, is where you are misinformed because the show to which you allude, namely Buffalo Bill's Wild West Show took place NEXT to the Owlerton Ground on Penistone Road! Me grandad went to see it, said it were champion."

"The show to which I what?"

"Allude, George me old Yorkshire Pudding, a word not commonly used or understood by the unwashed such as yourself."

"I heard there were a Red Indian got killed for real though," Harry said.

"Aye there were, he's buried somewhere in Sheffield they say. That were a different performance though, me grandad didn't see that."

"Poor chap, all them wars he went through in America and he cops it in Sheffield!"

Frank was dribbling round and round Stan's feet, "Come on Stanners, tha no better than Sam and he's got a funny foot!" But George put an end to his teasing by nipping between him and Stan, nicking the ball and hoofing it hard towards the goal. It stopped a yard short and Harry scooped it up and kicked it back out towards Stan. It was like kicking a lump of wood and when he headed it, Stanley didn't even watch where it went as he was too busy rubbing his head. "Chuff me that hurt, I'd sooner head that rock that bounced off your nut!"

"Flaming cheek," Harry yelled, "it was you that cobbed it!" They were mates again. George scampered after the ball and dribbled it skilfully towards the goal. He was sure to score but just as he was about to shoot Frank slid in from the side and legged him over in spectacular fashion. "Foxy's face!" shouted George, rubbing his shin.

"Tha what?" Frank said, "what's tha mean, 'Foxy's face?'"

"Foul!" said George, grinning.

"Good 'un! That's what we call 'em from now on! Foxy's face ref! A dirty Foxy's face!"

The next shot at goal ended in disaster for one of the pals and delight for the others as the ball landed in a big dollop of wet cow muck splashing stinking blobs of green slime all over the left goalpost which also happened to be Stanley's pullover. The three of them burst into laughter as poor Stan held it aloft, a look of dismay coupled with disgust on his face.

"Me nannan knitted that," he said then with a grin, "I think it's improved it, it's made a grand pattern. Want a bit?" and he whirled the thing round his head sending horrible smelly, green globules towards the others. The ball was forgotten as Stanley set off after them, careering from one to the other waving his pullover. They ran through the coarse grass and wild flowers in the sunshine until the heat and the giggles defeated them and they flopped down on their backs red in the face and gasping like beached fish. Harry sometimes came to this meadow on his own early on a summer morning before the hay was cut and lay on his back among the cowslips, pretty pink milkmaids and buttercups, the long grasses framing a patch of blue sky in which a lark was fluttering upwards until it was a black pin dot high above. The song seemed to be from the whole sky, trilling and fluting impossible arpeggios. Sometimes the little bird stayed singing at the pinnacle of its climb for as much as five minutes before drifting slowly down. Harry loved it when occasionally a bird stopped singing halfway to Earth, folded its wings and dropped like a stone the rest of the way. If he lay there long enough and held his nerve eventually the cows would wander over and form a jostling circle around him, overcome by curiosity. It was funny to lie there looking up at their startled faces with their gentle eyes and shiny wet noses as they let out the occasional startled "Huff" and lowered their woolly heads for a better look at this strange supine creature.

"Has he nodded off?" came Frank's voice, "Nah then, Sleeping Beauty are we finishing this game of togger or not?"

"Not," said Harry "I can't be bothered, it's too hot and one of the goalposts is all ovver cow muck."

One by one the boys sat up, leaning backwards on their hands, faces tilted towards the sun.

"It's grand this, isn't it?"

"It is that George. Grand weather, grand pals and Stanley's gansey all covered in cow plop; it doesn't get a lot better than that on a fine summer Saturday does it?"

"Gi'o'er Frank" Stan said, "I'm going to really catch it when I get home it's no laughing matter having a cow ploppy pullover to explain," but it was too late and they were soon all convulsed with painful giggles again.

At the field margin stood the lonely figure of a boy. Foxy was watching.

"What's happened to your face?" Laurie asked when Harry walked through the door at teatime, "you've a reight shiner."

"Nowt, just got elbowed playing togger. Is it turning black?"

"Mainly purple and red with a pleasing hint of yellow and maybe a splash of green," Laurie said. "You want to watch them mates of yours they're a reight rough bunch by t'looks of things."

Harry had the feeling that Laurie didn't really believe him but he was too good a brother to probe. If Harry didn't want to tell, then that was fine. Harry wasn't sure why he didn't want to tell his brother, it certainly wasn't for the shame of fighting, there was glory in that even if you lost. No, it was something to do with the look on Foxy's face when George's dad had hold of him and the wet patch on his trousers. That was something that shouldn't have happened and it troubled him though he couldn't really have explained why.

CHAPTER EIGHT:

July 1912

At his next rehearsal Harry arrived to find the little band room alive with a sense of feverish excitement. "What's up?" he asked John Fenwick.

"Haven't you heard? It's all over t'village."

"Heard what? I don't know what you're on about."

"It looks like t'King and Queen's invited 'emselves for a few ales and a spot of snap round at Billy Fitzbilly's little cottage and we've been asked to give 'em summat to listen to to stop 'em getting bored of an afternoon!"

Harry gaped at him, "You're joshing aren't you?" Billy Fitzbilly was the nick- name of the Earl William Fitzwilliam who lived at Wentworth Woodhouse a couple of miles away from Chapeltown geographically but an entire world away in terms of the way its inhabitants lived. The house was one of the largest private residences in the country and had so many rooms that even the owners didn't know how many there were; the only certainty was that there was at least one room for every day of the year. It sat in acres of parkland which were roamed by magnificent red deer and had a frontage that was longer than Buckingham Palace. There were lakes stocked with fish and woods bustling with glossy pheasants but woe betide anyone who thought of poaching there as the gamekeepers were known to be a rough lot armed with hefty cudgels. The family were fabulously wealthy because they had owned all the coalmines for miles around for as long as anyone could remember. "Billy" was thought of as a good and generous owner and employer though Harry's dad had once said, "Aye, generous if you think making men work underground for twelve hours a day for not much money then giving 'em a bit of a party once a year and letting 'em come in and have a gawp round your massive house as long as they don't touch owt or talk to t'posh folks is generous, then aye he's generous enough." Still, The King! Harry could hardly believe his ears. "Do you mean it? You're not having me on are you?"

"No lad, it's reight," said Robert Wildblood, "we've only just found out. Norman knew a few days ago but he were sworn to secrecy."

His eyes, which looked big at the best of times due to the thick lenses of his little round spectacles, were wide and earnest. Like everyone Harry knew, Bob Wildblood was a fervent royalist and admirer of the "quality" as the local aristocracy were known and used to relate with gusto how his father had had to jump into a ditch in Harley and tug his forelock as the Fitwilliam's yellow landau thundered by one day. These days they lorded it around the countryside in a bright yellow Rolls Royce motor car and Earl Billy was known to give people a cheerful wave as he passed by rather than trying to run them off the road.

"And we've to play? When is it?"

"Well here's t'best bit, he's arriving on t'eighth and we're to play on t'eleventh when they're having a bit of a do before they go home."

Harry never swore but on this occasion one of those words slipped out as he swooshed air out between his teeth.

"That's in a week!"

"Very good Mester Einstein, did you work that out all on your own?" John said.

"Mester who?"

"German chap, very clever, don't you worry your pretty little head about it. Point is they want t'junior band to play and t'big lads in t'main band aren't happy but it's hard cheese. Anyhow it's next week so we'd better crack on."

They rehearsed that night with such a sense of purpose, driven on by Mr Barnes who pushed and cajoled and became exasperated in equal measure, that by the end they were all exhausted and hurting but felt satisfied and happy that after a couple more sessions they'd be good enough for a king. Harry set out for home, his lip numb and swollen but with a spring in his step and a skip in his heart. His news was so immense that he couldn't wait to tell his ma and pa and Laurie and a grin began to creep across his face as he broke into a trot. He chuckled to himself, imagining their open-mouthed amazement when he told them what he had been chosen to do in just a few days' time. He upped his pace as he neared his house. It was a lovely warm evening so he wasn't surprised to see the front door open. The dappled clouds were flushed with dog rose pink and the summer's breath smelt of sweet honeysuckle and night scented stocks growing in the pretty cottage gardens. Harry was very happy, his world seemed perfect to him, full of love, happiness and music and now this great excitement was making him tingle. He burst into the kitchen and stopped before he could utter the first word. The room was empty.

"Mam ! Pa!" he yelled but no voices answered just the clattering sound of Laurie's boots pounding down the stairs from their room above. His face appeared round the door, pink and with a serious expression it rarely had.

"They're out, been gone more than an hour. They've gone to a meeting in t'parish hall. Said they might be out while ten o'clock."

"What about?" Harry said. He felt a bit deflated as he'd wanted to astound them with his incredible news and now he'd have to wait until they came home.

"Some chap from London's come to give a talk about summat; father said it were about when t'king comes and how we've all to behave if we get invited to t'big house."

"How come you know?" Harry said.

"Somebody put a note through t'door in a reight posh envelope, everybody got one! It's on t'side in t'kitchen if you want to have a look."

The envelope was a rich cream colour and had the royal crest embossed in the corner. Inside was a note requesting the occupants of the house to attend a meeting in the parish hall to be briefed about "His Majesty King George V and Queen Mary of Teck's visit to their loyal subjects in the Parish of Ecclesfield and surrounding villages." It was signed "Lord Knollys, Private Secretary to his Majesty The King."

"Well guess what," Harry said feeling a bit peeved that his thunder had been stolen, "We've been asked to play at t'tea party in front of the King and all t'quality."

"Have you? That's grand!" Laurie said, "I hope I can come and hear you." He wandered out into the garden pausing at the door to breathe in the scented evening air and Harry stood for a moment thinking and feeling a little ashamed. If he'd been Laurie he would have been jealous and probably said something dismissive or rude but Laurie wasn't made that way and Harry made a mental note to thank him later.

He went upstairs, took out his precious soprano cornet and pushing through the pain of his crushed lip, began to play. His bedroom window was open and as the silvery notes floated out into the evening on the warm air, neighbours out in their gardens, chatting over front gates or returning from the meeting, stood and listened as the moon rose over the roof tops and the crystal droplet of Venus heralded the coming night.

"Lovely, that," Cyril Slynne said to himself as he stood listening in his cottage doorway. It was overhung by a giant honeysuckle that, at this time of the evening was spilling its heavy perfume to mix with the myriad other flower scents from the gardens around, drugging the last lazy bees as they stumbled drunkenly from blossom to blossom. The pure, clear music threaded the top end of the village together, gilding the evening air with loveliness and Cyril, a lonely widower felt part of a shared moment and just a little less lonely when he thought of all the others who were listening too. Music can do that to the human spirit. Harry played on oblivious of the effect he was having until he heard the door bang downstairs as his parents came home.

In the kitchen Harry sensed an "atmosphere" and knew at once his mam and dad had had a rare disagreement about something.

Laurie raised his eyebrows as he passed Harry on his way up to their room and gave a little shrug of his shoulders as if to say "Grown-ups eh?"

Harry told his news quickly and went upstairs.

"What's up with them ? Have they fell out ?"

"Aye , it's funny though! I heard 'em before they went off to that meeting. Me mam said if t'king were coming she'd need a new hat and pa said t'king might have better things to look at than mam in a posh new hat so her church hat'd do just fine and he were only another posh chap and when were t'last time she asked for a new hat so she looked nice for him and anyway did she think money grew on trees? They had a reight barney and me mam called him a Bolshevik!"

"A what?" said Harry

"A Bolshevik! I don't know what it means but it sounds funny and it didn't please pa because he called her a flibbertigibbet and she threw a saucepan at his head! It were reight comical!"

The King spent the first day of the visit processing through the streets in an open topped car waving and smiling at the crowds of people who had gathered to catch a glimpse of him and Queen Mary. It was the most exciting thing that had ever happened and that night every household had a story of how the King had definitely smiled or waved especially at them. There was much happy discussion about how little he was compared to his wife who loomed above him in the car and how happy they had both looked but on the second day there was terrible news.

People starting their day near Cadeby Main Pit felt their cottages suddenly shake, tea cups on tables clattered like chattering teeth and seconds later a dull thud sounded, pushing against their windows like a heavy fist. Men setting off for the morning shift saw a terrible plume of black smoke and dust rise above the winding wheels of the pit head and knew at once what had happened. They began to run, banging on cottage doors as they went and calling men out to help. The news spread like a terrifying wave and within minutes a tide of men, women and children was flooding towards the mine. Women wrapped in shawls and clutching wailing children gathered together in their terror at the pit head waiting in horrified anticipation for news of their men. Underground in pitch darkness was a deafening stillness as those left alive by the huge explosion began to stir from where the blast had thrown them like puppets. Then the moaning and calling and scrabbling began. Gasping in the stench of firedamp they crawled blindly if they could, blinking coal grit from their eyes but seeing only darkness, spitting and trying to clear their clogged nostrils of the suffocating dust. Those who crawled or staggered in their disorientated confusion towards where the explosion had occurred met a solid wall of fallen rock where the collapsed roof met the ground and knew at once that there was no hope of survival from that place. In a gob, off the main road, two men, fumbling in the inky blackness, were trying to help a terribly broken man gagging and gasping at the wet stink of him and sobbing as he cried weakly out in his torment. All through that section of the pit were similar stories of death and agony and when the little metal tally checks were counted as men straggled to the surface there were more than thirty missing.

"We need men to volunteer for the rescue." Pit Deputy Harold West announced to the crowd at the pit top at two o'clock that afternoon and every man standing there feeling helpless in the enormity of the disaster stepped forward. Descending in the cage in three waves of twenty men they were met by the stifling stench of gas and dust and utter filthy darkness. Who knows what caused it, a piece of metal accidentally kicked against another? A pick striking an ironstone? But as they trudged forward and began to dig a spark flared and the scant air bloomed with another vast, orange explosion, then another and another and fifty three more families were without sons, fathers, brothers and husbands. When the final tally was taken ninety one men were never going home and in the early grey dawn their families straggled home to cottages to deal with their grief and fear of a now terrifyingly uncertain future.

It was assumed the royal visit would be ended but it wasn't and during the course of that terrible day the king and queen visited several pits to show they cared about their labouring subjects. The king even descended to the coalface at Elsecar and hewed coal in his shirtsleeves alongside the sweating colliers in amidst the dust and deafening roar of the machinery that wrenched the black diamonds from the earth making England great and wealthy. In Cadeby the queen shed tears with the grieving families and the king raised his hand to silence the subdued cheers of the small crowd who had turned out to see him, as a mark of respect for his dead and dying subjects. The bell of Wentworth church tolled in the early evening and Earl Fitzwilliam himself led a service, struggling to find words of comfort for the few who straggled in to listen and try to come to terms with the loss of fellow workers. Living in pit villages people knew the dangers of mining and a fear of death underground hung like a grey ghost in the background of their lives. Most people knew someone who had been lost or injured but this was on a terrible new scale and would be a great raw wound in their tight knit communities for generations to come.

Life and mining went on and when the final great day arrived the villages around the big house put on a grand show and there was a holiday atmosphere with bunting strung between the gas lamps and the Union Jack hanging from upstairs windows. At first people were a bit uncertain about celebrating, not wanting to appear disrespectful after the awful news but neighbour agreed with neighbour that what was done was done and they would continue to pull together to help those grieving afterwards so they were allowed to celebrate today. Earl Fitzwilliam had opened up the grounds of the big house and his coal mines were operating on short shifts so that most men had a chance to enjoy at least some of the day with their families. Harry's mam looked resplendent in her enormous new hat which was a confection of flowers and feathers that was so big it had to be held in place by a fistful of vicious looking hatpins and she clutched a posy of sweet-peas picked that morning. His pa was dressed in his only suit which was a little shiny but he had refused to buy a new one muttering darkly about silly hats that cost more than a day's pay when his wife had suggested a visit to the shops in Sheffield. The only concession he'd made was to polish his best boots to a mirror shine. He had spent a good hour the evening before warming the little tin of bootblack on the stove then spitting on his boots as he polished with a soft brush until they shone like glass. As they set off walking the three miles to Wentworth Harry thought they all looked grand. Laurie was in his best suit with smart new stockings that were held up with special tapes round the top that his mam had sewn with tiny Union Jack tabs at the side. At the moment he looked spick and span with his hair carefully parted in the middle and slicked down with sugar water but Harry knew that as soon as he met his mates and went running off into the deer-park surrounding the great house to play he'd look as dishevelled as he always did within minutes. For now though they all looked a picture. Harry's uniform was beautifully laundered and pressed and his boots matched his dad's for shine. The roads were already thronged with people and more were trickling into the general flow from cottages and gardens all heading in the same direction. There was an atmosphere of tingling anticipation and a great hubbub of excited chatter and the route was gay and colourful with the bunting and flags, that waved and fluttered in the gentle breeze, which were strung across the lanes from gas lamp to gas lamp. Everyone was in their Sunday best and a chorus of "God Save The King" broke out sporadically among the crowd adding to the patriotic fervour of the occasion. Harry felt a thump on his shoulder and turned expecting to see Frank or Sam or one of his other mates but to his surprise there was no one behind him.

"Were that you?" he said to Laurie whose shocked little face was the first thing he saw when he turned.

"No! it were Foxy, back of your jacket's a reight mess!" Harry squirmed an arm round and felt up the back of his uniform jacket. His fingers encountered a slimy mess of mud and grass. He spun around, Foxy was standing beside the road laughing and wiping his hands down the front of his jersey.

"Say hello to t'king for me!" he shouted before turning and shoving his way through the crowd.

"Well that's just flaming typical, why the hell can't he just leave me alone, me coat's ruined I hope Mr Barnes has got a spare," Harry said, fighting back hot tears of anger and frustration. Once again his day had been ruined by Robert Fox and he could think of no reason. His dad was too far in the distance talking to a neighbour to tell and anyway Harry didn't want to spoil his day so he trotted through the throng to find Mr Barnes and see if there was a spare jacket. There was but it had obviously belonged to a giant and an overweight one at that and it swamped him. Still there was nothing he could do so with a sigh, he rolled the sleeves up and went to find the rest of the band. At first one or two of the lads laughed but when he explained the reason they soon changed their tune and one or two of the bigger lads began talking about sorting Foxy out themselves. "Don't do that," Harry said, "You'll just make it worse, he'll blame me then all hell'll let loose." That wasn't the real reason though. That wet patch and the look in Robert Fox's eyes were the real reason.

Mr Barnes finally gathered the band together and they were unspeakably excited because they were placed just beside the massive, bronze front doors of the big house on the terrace right beside where the King and his entourage would emerge to wave to the crowds. Mr Barnes wagged his hands for quiet and hush descended eventually.

"I don't think I need to tell you boys, this is a big day for Chapeltown Silver Band, so play up and make us all proud. Now we're needed back here by eleven thirty prompt so go and enjoy yourselves until then. Don't overdo it and don't be late back and above all else keep your uniforms clean and tidy. Harry, I think I've another jacket at home so I'm going to nip and get it for you."

"It's all reight Mr Barnes I'll manage, you'll miss out on all t'fun if you have to walk home."

"Aye and you'll be as useful as a chocolate fire guard if you're not comfortable. You can't play properly if you're all wraxed up in that thing, I've one at home as'll fit you so I'll see you in a bit."

Harry watched his broad, slightly stooped back bustling through the crowd, his balding head shiny in the sunshine. He was a kind man, Norman Barnes. Harry knew it was a good hour's walk to his house and back and he also knew that he would have been enjoying a pint with his friends courtesy of Earl Fitzwilliam in one of the marquees that had been erected if he hadn't promised to help Harry so he felt a great wave of gratitude.

"Come on, let's get some snap," said a familiar voice beside him, making him jump. "You were away wi't'fairies there Harry old stick. Come on, get with it, there's no time to lose, there's comestibles to be had free, gratis and for nowt and growing lads like us need to stuff our faces by order of the king! I expect it's caviar and roast swan sarnies washed down by champagne"

"Hey up Frank, not seen you for a bit! Where's all t'others?"

"Douglas and Stan are in that big white tent. Not seen Sam yet but he said to meet him by t'gates at half ten. Come on there's some right snap to be had and they say you can have as much as you want!"

Unlimited food was a rarity in the boys' lives so they set off with a great sense of urgency, weaving their way between the hundreds of people all in their best clothes, smiling and chattering and with pretty china cups of tea or pots of beer in their hands. Children raced between legs and mothers shouted at them to stay clean or else, while fathers told them to leave them alone and let them have a good time as it wasn't every day the King came to Wentworth. There was a great crush in the marquee and it took them a couple of seconds to spot their friends in the stifling interior. Douglas looked smarter than he'd ever looked in a proper grown up tweed suit that was slightly too big for him. The sleeves covered his hands, the shoulders of the jacket drooped a little and the trousers pooled in great rumples of material over his boot tops and could have easily accommodated two Douglases but he still looked grand.

"Hey up Dougie boy! Where's tha got that bobby dazzler from? Tha looks like tha's on thi way to a funeral."

"Not far off the truth Frank," Stan said with a grin. "It were his grandad's. He kicked t'bucket last month. He had two suits. This is t'one they didn't bury him in."

"I'm in a dead man's second best suit!" said Douglas with a smile, looking down at himself.

"That's a bit strong Douglas," Harry said, shocked by the boys' jokey tone. The man was dead after all and this seemed a bit disrespectful, especially from Douglas.

"Gi'oer Harry, he were a reight laugh my grandpa, he'd think it was hilarious. I bet he's watching now laughing his head off."

They shoved and jostled their way to the front of the crowd until they reached the long trestle table where the food was laid out. At one end was a tall stack of plates decorated with a picture of the King and the words "To Commemorate the Royal Visit to Wentworth Woodhouse by his majesty King George V and his consort Queen Mary of Teck"

"Where the 'ell's Teck?" said Douglas.

"No idea but let's "teck" some of these sarnies," Harry said reaching out for a big handful and loading them onto his plate. There was ham and cheese and tongue and delicious pickle between thick cut soft white bread, great slabs of pork pie with eye wateringly hot mustard, seed cake and Bath buns, Eccles cakes and sweet iced Sally Luns. The boys gorged themselves and drank glass after glass of the lemonade that foamed in great metal jugs on the tables and was dispensed by cheerful ladies, harassed but jolly in their pinafores, perspiring and pink in the face but smiling and happy. The pall cast by the terrible tragedy just a couple of miles away still hung in the background but today was a chance for those not directly affected to push it away for a few happy hours.

The boys roamed from tent to tent eating and laughing and holding their full stomachs, groaning and telling each other they'd never had so much snap in their lives.

"Hey up, anybody got t'time?" Stan said, "What time are you blowing your bugle Harry?"

"Flamin' 'ell ! Half eleven, I nearly forgot, why what time is it?"

"I shall tell you Harold my friend," Douglas said gravely, fishing inside his jacket pocket. He extracted a large, battered silver pocket watch on a heavy chain.

"Grandad's?" asked Sam

"Aye, we found it stopped dead in his pocket after he passed."

"What ? At the exact time he died?" said Harry. He'd heard stories of this before and there was even a song called "My Grandfather's Clock" that the band played regularly which told that same story.

"No, he died at three in t'morning and it were stopped at nine, he'd just forgotten to wind it up, lazy old bugger," Douglas grinned, "it's five and twenty past eleven, you've got five minutes Harry. You'd better get your skates on, t'King's waiting on you, you can't keep royalty waiting they'll put you in t'Tower!"

"Reight I'm off!" Harry said grabbing one last fairy cake from the nearest table and scooting through the jostling crowd.

He reached the terrace in front of the house with just a few seconds to spare and there was a smiling, perspiring Norman Barnes with a jacket slung over his arm. "Here you are lad, I just made it back in time, this should be a better fit."

It was perfect and immediately Harry felt ready to play. It was amazing what the uniform did, almost like becoming another person.

"Thanks Mr Barnes it's grand, fits like a glove."

"No thanks necessary Harry lad, just play like you've never played before."

"I will, I promise I'll not let you down."

The band had just settled into their wooden folding chairs, shuffled their music into place and tuned up when they heard a discrete cough and a liveried equerry nodded to them before solemnly opening the great doors of the house. Mr Barnes gestured and the boys stood, holding their instruments vertically in front of their chests all eyes on the doorway. There was a flurry of activity just visible inside the houses as equerries and ladies in waiting organised themselves into a guard of honour leading to a dainty table laid with a sparkling silver tea service and a cake stand holding tiny cakes and then they were there. The King was shorter than Harry expected and his consort, wearing heels was taller than him. Harry felt a twinge of disappointment as his Majesty was in a grey tweed suit and wearing a brown bowler hat and red and black neck tie. He'd been imagining a crown and cloak trimmed with ermine. Nonetheless it was The King himself! Queen Mary looked every inch the queen in an opulent cream costume with black velvet cuffs and a great wide brimmed hat decorated with huge camellias of pink and deep red. The royal couple paused at the top of the steps leading to the terrace where the band waited and the king raised his hand in greeting to the crowd who broke spontaneously into a chant of "God save the King! God save the King!" He gave a small nod and the couple descended to their waiting table.

"This is it boys," said Mr Barnes gesturing for them to be seated, "Myfanwy" and not too loud, we don't want to deafen them."

"Myfanwy" was a lovely old Welsh tune that was a staple of the brass band repertoire so the lads hardly needed to look at their music, concentrating instead on Norman Barnes' gently sweeping hands as he conducted with a beatific smile on his face. They played a blinder and Harry couldn't have been happier. The instrument felt like a part of him and every note came clear and true soaring over the rich tones of the band in a seemingly effortless stream. They played another four rousing tunes and it was only after they finished with a crashing crescendo at the end of the National Anthem that he felt the throb in his lip and the ache in his belly from the muscular control of his diaphragm. Playing quietly was a rare skill for brass players but they'd managed it and managed it well. Afterwards the King and Queen stood, gave the band a brief bow, waved to the crowd of onlookers and were whisked back inside amongst the kaleidoscope of liveried servants.

An audible sigh escaped the band and Mr Barnes stood gently clapping and beaming at them.

"Well done lads, you've done yourselves proud, that was grand. Happen we can put "By Royal Appointment" on our stand covers now! Come on let's pack down and you can go and enjoy yourselves, there's still a few hours before they chuck us out."

Harry was just blowing the spit out of his instrument and was about to give it a little polish with his soft yellow duster before putting it away when a voice said, "Are you Harry Jones?"

He jumped and turned round and found himself looking at a tall young man in the green and gold Fitwilliam livery with its shiny buttons sporting crowns and dragons. "Erm, yes I am," he stuttered.

"Come with me lad and make sure you're smart, there's somebody wants to meet you." He gave Harry a theatrical wink and brushed a bit of cotton from the shoulder of his jacket. "Bring that with you," he said, pointing at Harry's cornet, "he might want a look at it!"

He strode off without giving Harry time to ask any questions and stood, his hand on the great bronze door knob of the main door at the top of the stone steps. "Come on sonny Jim, we haven't got all day!" Harry trotted up the steps and the man swung the door open and ushered him inside. To say Harry had never seen anything like it was an enormous understatement. He was standing in a vast salon where the ornate ceiling was supported by sixteen huge pinkish stone pillars; in niches in the walls were white marble statues of classical figures, fabulous paintings hung on the walls and ornate gilded furniture was tastefully grouped around the central, open part of the room. The floor was a marvel of intricate marble marquetry polished to gleaming perfection in colours of pink, yellow and white. "Nice eh?" the young man said, "Come on, this way!" He stomped off ahead towards a grand, carpeted staircase as wide as Harry's whole house, turned left and knocked discretely at a heavy panelled door. A muffled voice said, "Come!"

The King was sitting in his shirtsleeves in a red overstuffed armchair beside a roaring fire. He looked tired and had enormous bags under his eyes but he looked delighted when he saw Harry standing in the doorway.

"Call him "sir"," the footman whispered, ushering Harry in before silently withdrawing and closing the door. Harry stood on trembling legs looking at the little bearded man seated in front of him.

The King smiled and said, "I don't bite sonny, come over here and let's have a look at you!" Harry could barely understand what he had said because he spoke in a way he had never heard anyone else speak, as if he had a mouth full of pebbles but he took a step towards him.

"Harry is it? Good old English name, been a few Harrys in my family," he said with a smile, "and what kind of a trumpet is that you were playing?"

"It's a sop sir,"

"Well what the dickens is one of those? I've never heard of a "sop! Is that its real name?"

"Soprano cornet sir, it's quite a new instrument. Everyone calls it a sop for short."

"Well bless my soul! It makes a grand sound, very sweet," The king said, his eyes twinkling.

"Thank you your majesty," Harry blurted.

"Sir will do," he said with a smile and Harry blushed to the roots of his hair.

"Come on then, let's have a look at it and then perhaps you might play a bit for me."

Heart pounding Harry sprang the catches and lifted the little gleaming cornet from its velvet bed. The King stretched out a hand and Harry put the instrument into it. "My word, it's tiny! What a lovely thing, how do I hold it?" Harry mimed where the fingers sat but the King made a hash of it and gestured for Harry to place his fingers in the right places. Harry gently lifted his fingers and positioned them correctly; he'd never felt skin so soft, even his mam's hands roughened and toughened by washing and scrubbing felt more manly. Harry couldn't believe what he was doing; it was like some kind of strange dream and the King picked up on it.

"I'd like to wager you didn't expect to be doing this today eh lad?"

"No sir, it is a bit ….." Harry searched for the word, "surprising!"

There was a pause during which Harry's legs turned to mush, had he said something to offend the King of England? Then the King let out a roar of laughter, tilting his head back and dabbing at his eyes with a monogrammed handkerchief. "Surprising! Bless my soul! I suppose it is a little surprising! By Jove yes, surprising!" The thing that surprised Harry the most was that he found it so funny, to Harry's way of thinking he'd just told the truth but the King's hilarity was catching and soon he was laughing along.

When he'd recovered a little of his breath the King said, "Can I blow it?"

"Of course sir just let me put the mouth piece in."

The royal lips were pursed and pressed to the mouthpiece and he blew as hard as he could and miraculously a long clear note wavered out into the room. He looked as shocked as Harry and when he'd run out of breath and the note had died he laughed again and shook Harry firmly by the hand. "Stop while you're ahead, that's my motto," he chuckled and handed the instrument back, "Let's hear the expert then, what can you play me?"

"Well I could play God Save The King if you'd like sir."

"Good grief boy, don't play that old dirge! I hear that far too often, play me something I can tap my foot to!"

"Well I do know one with a royal connection sir, how about "I'm Hennery The Eighth I am, I am"?"

"Perfect! Play away my boy!" He sat back in his chair, pressed the tips of his fingers together, smiled and nodded for Harry to begin.

There was a strict rule in the band that music hall songs were not to be played but this was by royal command so Harry launched joyfully into it and soon the King was clapping along and tapping the shiny shoes that peeped out from underneath gleaming white spats.

"Well done sonny that was absolutely splendid, now off you go. Here, take this as a memento." In his hand was a fresh white handkerchief with the royal arms embroidered in a corner. "Now you'll think of me and remember the day you played for the King of England every time you blow your nose!" He roared with laughter again, then stood up, shook Harry's hand firmly and gave a funny, stiff little bow before turning and walking out of the room through a door which seemed to open magically as he approached it. Harry stood for a moment wondering if the bizarre little interlude had been real or some kind of mad dream then packed his cornet away. The young man appeared again and beckoned to Harry from the doorway "Come on then, let's have you, not a bad old cove is he?"

"No, he's grand," Harry said, smiling, "quite funny actually, we had a right laugh and he gave me this!" He held out the handkerchief and the young man took it, examined the royal crest then made a great show of pretending to blow his nose on it. When Harry didn't laugh he said, "Suit yourself!" and handed it back before ushering Harry through the grand hall and back out into the noise and colour of the grandest party Wentworth Woodhouse had ever seen. Within seconds he was surrounded by a pushing gaggle of people all wanting to know what had happened and by the evening when the party came to an end Harry must have told his story a hundred times so by bed time he was exhausted. He flopped onto his bed and the last thing he heard before falling into a deep sleep was Laurie saying, "Well done our Harry, best pals wi' t'King, not a bad day's work!"

The hot summer days rolled by; days of making dens in the Barley fields, daring each other on a rope swing slung over a high branch of a huge sycamore , football and attempts at cricket in the cow field, lying laughing together in the long grass and marvelling at the sight of a blush of scarlet where poppies had bloomed in profusion in a freshly ploughed field in the distance.

One morning before dawn Harry called for Sam and Douglas and the three lads walked the four miles to the wild moorland of Wharncliffe Chase and as they sat on a rocky outcrop, an early morning red deer stag with his harem of hinds rose from the deep heather and bracken where they had lain all night, shaking crystal droplets of dew from his antlers sparkling into the breaking light before scenting the boys and trotting away to the cover of the nearby woodland. They held their noses high and seemed to move in slow motion. None of the boys moved or spoke until the last of the white flags of the deer's rear ends vanished between the trees then Douglas broke the silence with his usual flare for Yorkshire understatement, "Well that were all right weren't it?"

It was a summer like that.

Bobby Gregory never recovered from his fever and the village was consumed by sadness at the end of July. Harry passed his house the day they closed all the curtains and felt terrible. Since the Whit Marches he had been playing Soprano Cornet in Bobby's seat and playing it well but always assuming that Bobby would resume his place in the band as soon as he was well. Now he felt that he'd stolen something precious from him and was overwhelmed by guilt. The instrument he'd borrowed from Oughtibridge had long since been returned and once the danger of infection had passed Bobby's cornet had been placed in his hands. He tried to hand it to Mr Barnes after Bobby's passing but the lads in the band would have none of it.

"What do you think Bobby would have wanted to happen?" John Fenwick asked him gently, "Do you think he'd have wanted his chair to be empty and silent? This band needs a sop player, it's what gives us the edge."

"Aye I know, but it doesn't seem right, I feel bad for his family, it's like I've sneaked in when he was so badly, and now…" He couldn't finish without crying so he shut up and looked at the ground.

A note from Bobby's mother and father changed his mind. The little cornet had lain silent in its case for two weeks and Harry had gone back to playing his Bb instrument but with little heart. They were rehearsing in the sweltering band room one evening when the door creaked open and a thin little woman dressed all in black, with a dark bonnet and a black net veil obscuring her face edged in. She sat quietly at the back of the room until they had finished the piece they were playing then gestured for Mr Barnes to go to her. There was a murmured conversation, the briefest of handshakes then she was gone. Mr Barnes composed himself and said,

"That was Mrs Gregory boys. She wanted you to know that their Bobby passed quietly in his sleep but before he did, when he was first poorly, he talked about the band. He wanted to say well done.." his voice faltered and he had to pause to recompose himself. "He wanted to say well done for the Whit Marches. Mrs Gregory said you were all a grand bunch of lads; the best mates he could have had and she wanted you to have this Harry."

He held out a little white envelope. In spidery black ink was written "To Harry Jones" and the note inside said, "Take Bobby's seat with our blessing Harry Jones. Play on and play up." It was signed Mr and Mrs W Gregory. Harry never found out who had told them he'd tried to quit but the note made him determined to honour Bobby's memory by being the best he could be.

CHAPTER NINE:

Christmas 1913

"Where are you tonight? I might walk down with you if you're close I could do with a drink."

Harry's dad looked tired out; his face was pale and he'd taken to groaning when he lifted himself out of his chair by the fire. There was no snow yet but it had been bitterly cold for days and Harry's dad had barely seen daylight for several weeks as all the men at William Green and Co. were expected to work over time.

"We're at t'Black Bull . It should be a good one because they're singing an'all."

"Reight, I'll walk you down, just let me get my coat and cap."

His dad had been a bit guarded when Harry asked him why he had to do so much overtime but eventually it had come out .

"Bloody government lad, they're building ships like there's no tomorrow and they all need ovens."

"Why?"

"Nay don't ask me, it's summat to do wi' t'Germans; they're doing t'same and our lot's getting worried, I don't know. Our lot's building Dreadnoughts and God knows what they're up to. Upside is I'm earning a bit more so we can have a grand Christmas." He walked across the kitchen to the foot of the stairs and shouted, "Our Laurie, Harry's playing at t'Black Bull in a bit , are you coming?"

The Christmas brass band concerts and "sings" of locally written carols were the one time of the year when children were tolerated in pubs as long as they didn't drink alcohol and Harry was looking forward to this one. Laurie called down that he would come and thundered down the stairs. He was just putting his muffler on when Harry's mum walked in from the parlour where she'd been trimming up with paper chains.

"Where are you off to? Off on a beano without your old mother?"

Before they could answer she did it for them, "I know, it's t'Christmas sing in t'Black Bull tonight and I'm just a woman so I'm supposed to stay washing pots and sewing your socks here while you lot are gallivanting and having a grand time, well you can think again because I'm coming with you. You've had your tea, t'pots are washed and sided and t'parlour's trimmed up so I've time on my hands, besides I've already arranged to meet Mavis Cartwright there. Some of them carols have parts for women to sing and there's a group of us going to do it this year. Come on then, let's get going, I don't want to be first through t'door, you know what they'll say."

Harry's dad gaped at her dumbfounded. Women in the tap rooms of the local public houses were severely frowned upon but there was little use arguing. Mrs Jones had that steely glint in her eye again which meant there was no use objecting and she was striding through the door pinning her best hat in place as she went. Harry's dad exchanged a look with the boys, shrugged, closed his mouth and followed her out. He felt uneasy but quickly caught her up and linked her arm; they'd walk in together and God help anyone who said anything about it. It might not sit easy with him but he was a very loyal husband and he admired her nerve.

The gas lamp lighter was just finishing his rounds, his long pole with its little spirit lamp over one shoulder and his triangular ladder over the other. The lamps were casting their greenish pools of light all along Jonnywham Lane but there was no moonlight so in the gaps between the lamps it was pitch black and Laurie ran ahead and twice leapt out at the rest of them from the deep shadows with a ghoulish yell making them jump.

"Now then Alf, how's it going?" Harry's dad asked the lamplighter.

"Not bad," the old man replied, "it's perishing though. I've done all but this 'un then I'm off home for my tea. I might pop in to t'Black Bull later to listen to your lot playing Harry, they tell me you're a bit special on that trumpet of yours."

Harry blushed to the roots of his hair and his dad said, "Aye he's not bad Alf we're proud of him."

Harry was amazed, his dad hardly ever praised him, never mind in front of other people. He always said he didn't want Harry getting big headed and the most he ever gave was a grunted, "All reight that," whenever he heard him play. To hear his dad say he was proud was a big moment and Harry was suffused with warmth and love though he wouldn't have been able to tell you what it was.

"He's playing wi' t'big lads now you know."

"Aye so I heard," Alf said

Harry was promoted to the full band when he began to win first prize places at various local musical festivals and though he was by far the youngest player he was one of the best and the men respected him, though it had meant their practises were less fun as they had to mind their language and avoid rude jokes.

The Black Bull was thronged and Harry could hear the band beginning to tune up in the back room as he walked through the front door.

"We're a bit early," he said. It was seven thirty and the sing wasn't due to start until eight.

"We want a good spot," his mum said. She pushed open the door into the back room and they were met by a fug of yellowish tobacco fumes from all manner of clay pipes and cigarettes as thick as a peasouper fog. The noise of the men tuning up and the chatter of the singers who had already arrived suddenly stopped and a host of faces turned to face them. Pints stopped halfway to mouths, looks were exchanged and a heavy silence descended as the gathered men tried to grasp what they were seeing. Women who frequented the village pubs were known among the men as "pudding burners" because if they were there then they must have left their proper place in the kitchen preparing Yorkshire puddings for the men folk and must have left them in the oven to burn. It was a joke but it held a strong grain of belief that many of the men held.

"I see I'm t'first then," Harry's mum said.

"You and your old man want t'front parlour love," said an elderly man from across the room.

"No, Nathaniel Salt, I do not want the front parlour, there's a few of us ladies singing tonight and you'd better get used to it, times are changing so you can stop calling me love for a start."

Nathaniel or "Flappy" as he was known on account of his huge ears opened his mouth to speak but Harry's dad cut in, "Careful what you say Flappy, she's here with my blessing and even if she wasn't you'd better get used to it because there's some others coming an' all so clear a corner for 'em."

There was a bit of a rumble of discontent and a little laughter but one by one the men shuffled round until a few tables in the corner of the room had been vacated and Harry's mum sailed imperiously across the room settling her broad bottom down, taking her hat off and fluffing her skirts out to get comfortable. "Right, I think I could enjoy a port and lemon if you wouldn't mind father," she said to Harry's dad and he disappeared in the direction of the bar. Harry pottered over to the band and said, "Sorry about that but she would come."

"Nay Harry, I'm glad she did, some of these carols have descants and soprano parts, it's about time we had someone to sing them properly instead of some of these silly old fools busting a gut thinking they're Caruso trying to hit top notes," Bernard Grant replied, twiddling the valves of his tuba.

With a great rustling of best silk skirts and much laughter at the shocked faces of some of the men, the rest of the women arrived until the corner was packed and a convivial atmosphere of banter and warmth began to settle on the room. Harry smiled to himself. His mother worked so hard to keep them all well fed and looked after and she often looked exhausted and careworn so it was lovely to see her laughing raucously with the other women and getting a little bit tipsy on port and lemon for once.

He unclipped the case of his brand new soprano cornet which had been presented to him by Mr Barnes after Chapeltown Silver band had won an area competition earlier that year and his playing had been singled out for particular praise by the adjudicators. Bobby Gregory's instrument had been presented to an up and coming player in the junior section. He still got a tingle when he opened the little leather box and saw the beautiful shiny little instrument winking up at him from its soft black velvet interior. "Reight, let's show 'em," he murmured half to himself but also half to the cornet. He glanced up, thank goodness no one had heard him they'd think he was a right soft lad if they caught him talking to it!

"Ladies and gentlemen," Mr Barnes called out above the hubbub, clacking a spoon against a pint pot, "We'll be playing in about half an hour so just give us a bit of hush to tune up for a minute."

The noise died quickly down, Mr Barnes was a respected figure in the three villages, Ecclesfield, Grenoside and Chapeltown from which the band drew its members.

One by one the musicians began to hit their note and out of the cacophony a magical harmony began to emerge as Mr Barnes pointed at individual members and gestured up or down with his baton to indicate whether they were sharp or flat.

"That'll do lads, we're kicking off in half an hour so you can get a drink, but just the one mind!"

Harry left his cornet on his chair and wandered away to find his dad. This was the bit he didn't like about being in the senior band as the men didn't really want him joining in their adult conversations about wives and sweethearts, work and politics so he often just went into a corner on his own and read a book or did a bit of extra practise. Tonight was different though as his mother and father and Laurie were here. Laurie had met up with some pals and they were off somewhere in the churchyard opposite the pub messing about among the tomb stones daring each other and playing hide and seek and his mother was leaning back in her seat, pink in the face and gasping with laughter at some filthy comment one of the women had made about her husband.

Harry's dad was leaning against the bar deep in conversation with some of his work mates and Harry crept closer to listen. Stuart Grange was talking animatedly and the other men were nodding their agreement from time to time. "It's gone on too long now, summat needs doing," Stuart said, slopping a wave of beer over the side of his tankard as he plonked it on the bar for emphasis, "What's up with them that they have to be so flaming belligerent all t'time? I don't get what it's got to do with us ovver here in this country anyway."

"I know, but they're starting to want to be top dog and that's not on. I read in t'paper that they're claiming a bit of France belongs to them and they're wanting it back." Harry's dad said.

"That's as maybe but why do they want all these ships built? They've thousands and thousands joined their navy you know, summats bubbling and our bloody government's keeping it under their 'ats."

"It's him, old Kaiser Willy that's at t'back of this, looking out for his Austrian mates even though he's part of our royal family."

"Cousins or summat aren't they? I know he's one o' t'old queen's grandkids, she must be spinning in her grave like a top, it's not reight what's going on and we'll be t'poor buggers that cop for it if summat kicks off; he needs teaching a lesson."

It was all confusing gobbledegook to Harry but he had noticed his dad had been spending far more time buried in his newspaper of an evening, occasionally tutting loudly or letting out a long drawn out exasperated sigh and chucking his reading glasses onto the table. When Harry asked him what was wrong he just dismissed it and said something about politics and "The flaming Boche getting too big for their boots" before turning the conversation to something else. He was a bit more short-tempered than usual but Harry just put it down to tiredness because of all the overtime he was putting in.

"Do you want summat to drink young 'un?" said Stuart when he noticed Harry lingering at the edge of the group, "How old are you now son?"

"I'm thirteen Mr Grange," Harry replied.

"Oh, tha can't have a pint of ale then, what have you got for a young 'un Johnny?" He called to the barman.

"Nowt, he'll have to have Adam's ale if he wants owt!" said the barman, a big, surly fellow with his black hair Brilliantined and plastered to his head either side of a knife sharp central parting. "We don't usually hold with kids in this boozer." He turned his back on them, muttering his irritation to himself.

"Aye and season's greeting to you an' all you grumpy old bugger, anybody'd think we'd asked him for a gold pig!" Stuart said before turning back to Harry and pressing a threepenny bit into his hand. "T'beer off's only round t'corner on Stocks Hill Harry, go and get yourself some lemonade or summat." Harry didn't really want to leave the cosy, grown up warmth of the pub with its intoxicating aromas of tobacco and ale but he couldn't say no as Mr Grange thought he was doing him a favour and threepence was threepence after all. He could get himself some mint humbugs with that as well as a drink. As he stepped out of the front door of the pub he could hear Laurie and his friends making silly ghost noises in the churchyard and it struck him how the two years between them was beginning to make a difference. He and his friends rarely had that kind of fun anymore especially now that one or two of the older lads had left school and started their apprenticeships in the steel works. He felt a pang of regret and briefly thought he might run up the steps and through the lych-gate to join in the game but thought better of it and headed left up church street towards Woodcock's beer off. The sky was the colour of buffed lead and he took a long sniff; they said you could smell snow coming but all he could smell was the reek of coal smoke as people's fires were stoked and banked to warm their cottages for the coming night. It had turned bitterly cold though and a North wind was whooping down the gennels and snickets of the village causing him to pull his cap hard down on his head and hoik his jacket tight across his chest. He opened the door of Woodcock's beer off shop and tall, thin Mr Woodcock appeared through the curtain that led to his back kitchen scratching his sparse, greasy hair and wrapping his apron round him, "Nah then young 'un what can I get you?"

"I've got threepence," Harry said, "what can I get as well as some lemonade?"

"A quarter of anything from the bottom row of jars, mixed or separate."

Harry ran his eyes along the row of big glass jars. There were stripy mint humbugs, lemon drops, bullseyes, beautiful smooth white mint imperials, little wrinkled tiger nuts and yellowish sticks of licorice and perhaps most tempting of all, giant white gobstoppers that had to be taken out of your mouth every so often to examine what colour they had changed to as you sucked each layer off. There wasn't enough time for gobstoppers; they needed a solid commitment so Harry asked for a mix of humbugs, mint imperials and bullseyes. Mr

Woodcock flicked a white paper bag open and shovelled a few of each sweet in before popping the bag on the scales.

"That's exactly twopence worth and a penny for your lemonade Harry."

Harry handed him the coin, took the bag and offered one to Mr Woodcock before popping a humbug in his mouth.

"Thanks Harry, don't mind if I do, oh and here, I reckon you might enjoy one of these later." He took down the jar of gobstoppers and fished one out."

"On me son, now go and make some noise wi' that bugle o' yours!"

"Thanks Mr Woodcock, thanks a lot!" said Harry through a mouthful of humbug. He might look a bit seedy but Mr Woodcock was a kind man who loved his brass band music.

Half an hour later, back in the snug , thick air of the back room of the Black Bull where the landlord had grudgingly lit a fire, the first carol was starting. Ike Baxter, Caesar's father, was master of ceremonies and he'd announced that the first was to be "A Song For The Time When The Sweet Bells Chime" a lovely local composition which Mr Barnes had carefully arranged for the band. The introduction filled the room with its sweet melody and the voices swelled into the warmth, made so much better this year by the addition of the soaring alto and soprano parts of the women creating a magical contrast to the men's rumbling tones.

Harry loved every second, especially after Laurie came in, red faced and sticky haired from his exertions and brazenly joined the ladies' corner, adding his clear, fluting treble voice to the choir. He gave Harry a cheeky wink as if to say, "I don't give a fig what anybody says, I'm having a sing with my mam!"

It was all over too quickly when the Landlord clanged the brass bell above the bar and shouted "Last orders at the bar gentlemen PLEASE." He made a great point of stressing the word "gentlemen" and glowered heavily over at the women some of whom gave him a cheeky wave or a wink. He grunted in annoyance and turned back to polishing glasses. He'd get used to the new times eventually but for now women in tap rooms were a shock to his system. When the final pints had been downed and "We wish you a merry Christmas" with its stomach rumbling talk of figgy pudding had been played and sung the room began to empty. "Well done everybody there was some grand playing tonight," Mr Barnes said from behind his thick yellow muffler, "you gave the ladies something to latch onto Harry, very nice!"

"Aye, grand work son," one of the trombone players added smiling over at Harry.

Harry's mum and dad and Laurie were saying last goodbyes and "Merry Christmases" to a gaggle of people near the fire as Harry joined them. One or two of the adults said well done then they headed out into the night. The sky had begun to shed fat fairy snow-flakes which were lazily drifting through the lamp light and the road was already covered in a fluffy carpet. Across the way the glow of advent candle light made the ancient stained glass church windows with their stories of knights and saints, luminous and utterly beautiful and the church, standing high above the road, wore a white cap as if it too was about to settle down to sleep. Little pillows of snow were building on the tombs and gravestones of slumbering generations long gone and the family paused in the middle of the road to gaze in silence for a while. Laurie spoke first, "Sledging tomorrow after school if it settles!" Harry caught his excitement and thrusting his cornet case into his dad's hands he bent and scooped a handful of snow. Laurie was no fool, he recognised a snowball when he saw one and ran, slithering and slipping on smooth boot soles up the road bending and scooping as he went, to make his own. Whooping and shouting, the boys hurled snowballs at each other until a big one from Laurie whizzed past Harry's ear and caught their mother square in the chest. "Tha's done it now Harry Jones," Laurie shouted.

"Ey up ! It was you that chucked it," Harry squeaked in outrage.

"I don't care who chucked it, you little buggers but I won't have it!" their mother shouted and the two boys dropped their missiles and stood sheepishly awaiting the inevitable clips around their ears. But a shock was in store as their mam suddenly pounded handfuls of snow together and began to hurl rock hard snowballs with deadly accuracy at them, shrieking with laughter. Their dad joined in after plonking Harry's cornet case on the church wall and in a few short seconds a full- blown snowball battle was underway. "I was a lass once you know!" their mum shouted as a beauty caught Laurie right on the back of his head sending a cascade of powdery snow down the back of his neck, "Don't ever underestimate the power of a mam who's been hit by a snowball!" The boys scooted up through the church lychgate and ran from hiding place to hiding place behind the ancient grey and green gravestones, popping up to pepper their ma and pa with snowballs whooping and shouting every time they scored a hit and squealing with hilarity when they copped for one. Their fingers were numb with cold when they eventually got home but their hearts were warm with love and family togetherness. All that and sledging tomorrow! just boring school to get through first. As they snuggled under their eiderdowns Harry and Laurie smiled in the dark and listened to their parents' voices from the downstairs kitchen punctuated by occasional bursts of laughter until they both slipped into contented sleep.

Three hours later Harry woke with a sickening lurch; something in his subconscious dreams had told him his cornet was not with him when he'd come through the door. It was a befuddled moment or two before he worked out where it was. His dad had put it on the church wall when the snowball fight broke out and that was where it still was. He had to get it before it was completely ruined if it wasn't already. He burned with shame; how could he have been so careless? He swung his legs over the edge of the bed dreading the icy moment when his bare feet hit the linoleum. Luckily he'd just stepped out of his clothes and he found them crumpled beneath his feet when he stepped down. There was no point taking his warm nightshirt off so he crammed it into his trousers, tugged on his stockings and a warm woollen jumper. His jacket and boots were downstairs in the kitchen and he needed to creep as quietly as he could so as not to wake the rest of the family. Outside was a silent, cushioned world lit a pale blue by a full moon. The snow clouds had drifted north and there was a crunch and diamond sparkle to the surface of the freezing snow as Harry made the first footsteps away from the house. His breath caught in his throat as he breathed the freezing air in and made soft smoke when he breathed out. It was the best part of a mile back to the church and the snow was knee deep so the going was hard but Harry began to enjoy the adventure as he ploughed onwards. There was a muffled silence to the lane and not a single person was out; it was his world for as long as the journey took. The physical effort of plodding through the snow which had drifted above knee height in places soon warmed him and he even began to regret the extra layer of his nightshirt which had ruckled uncomfortably around his middle, but his nannan had always said he must keep his kidneys warm to avoid certain death in cold weather so he was not going to un-tuck it from his trousers. He stumped onwards, whistling from time to time to allay the loneliness and mild apprehension he felt until after half an hour the church hove into view and he upped his pace. "Still be there, still be there, still be there," he chanted inside his head as he rounded the top of Church Street and headed down the sloping road to where he remembered his father leaving his cornet. It was there; a vague hump under the wall's thick white cap and he sighed with relief but there was something else, a partially covered humped, shadowy shape a little further down the road from his cornet, nestled at the foot of the wall, showing black patches through a covering of snow. Harry stopped, his heart lurching as he tried to make sense of it. He moved closer, one hand unconsciously scooping his cornet case from beneath the snow as he passed. It was a man lying prone on his side facing the church wall. He was wearing a heavy black coat and was capless and snow had settled in his hair. He was terrified but Harry crept closer, "Mister, mister!" No reply came. Harry looked round. Every cottage was dark and silently sleeping under their snow mufflers so he took another step. "Mister!" Nothing. He took a deep breath and reached out a hand to shake the man's shoulder. The movement made the figure roll backwards and with a horrible shock Harry realised he was looking straight down at the face of his friend George's father and in the next second Harry realised he was dead. His eyes were wide open and frozen white like chalk pebbles and in amongst grizzled grey whiskers his mouth hung open in the midst of its last ever breath like a horrible black cave. With a little cry Harry stumbled backwards and sat heavily in the snow, then scrambling to his feet, gasping and sobbing he began to run towards the nearest cottage across the road. He pounded hard on the door shouting and shouting for help until after a seeming age he heard a bolt being drawn on the other side and an old man's voice calling, "Whisht, whisht, what the bloody hell's a matter?"

"He's dead!" was all he could manage in between great sobs, "he's dead."

The door opened and an elderly man clutching a candle stood there. He was dressed in a night shirt and white bed hat topped with a red silken tassel .

"What the hell are tha' doin' out at this time young 'un ?"

Harry couldn't speak but stood aside and looked across the street. The old man followed his gaze and saw the huddle of black and white. "What is it?" he said lifting his candle.

"It's George's dad and he's dead mister."

"What you on about lad? George who?"

"Mr Fletcher, it's George's pa, he's stiff and his eyes are open and I think he's dead."

"Nay, nivver, come in t'house I'd better have a look."

He steered Harry gently into the kitchen and sat him down in an armchair beside a fire where the embers were still glowing red. Harry sat in stunned silence, his cornet case dripping melting snow across his knees. The old man left the room only to reappear a few moments later swathed in a thick dressing gown fastened with a silk cord. He pulled gumboots on and set out across the lane shutting the door behind him. Harry sat in the quiet of the dark kitchen accompanied by the heavy tick of a grandfather clock until the door reopened and the old man stepped in, his face drawn and sad. "I know him, silly bugger'll have fallen down drunk." There was both sadness and kindness in his voice for though he was a sad drunk, George's father was thought of in the village as a tragic figure and many could remember the kind, funny man he had been before he was overtaken by the cruel twist which had destroyed him.

"Those poor bairns, first their mother and now this," the man said. "You wait here lad while I get dressed. I'll take you home then I'd better get Mester Fairthorne out to see to that poor devil." Fairthorne was the undertaker, there was no point fetching Dr Frazer it was too late.

Harry never saw his best friend George or his sister, little Sarah again. There was talk that they'd gone to live with relatives in Halifax but Harry feared something much darker had become of them because he saw a horse drawn coach leaving The Lanes a few mornings after, driven by a grim- faced man in a black coat and tall hat and he wasn't sure but he thought he saw the word "orphans" on the side. The pathetic little house fell into disrepair and no one went near it as its sad atmosphere was too much to bear for some and others feared the ghosts that lived there now.

The day after his grim discovery Harry went to school as usual; there was no reason not to; it wasn't his father. He found he was suddenly of interest to everyone. Within minutes of walking through the wrought iron gates with their Latin motto he was surrounded.

"Where was he?"

"What did he look like?"

"They say he was stiff as a board"

"Was he murdered?"

"What were tha doin' out at that time?"

"What did you do?"

"Is he still theer? I'm going for a look if he is."

There was no time to answer before the next question came at him so he just pushed through the struggling throng and walked straight back out of the gates. Not one single one of them had asked about his best mate George. He headed towards The Lanes hoping to see him but there was a bobby on duty outside the door of the house and the scraps of material that served as curtains were drawn across the filthy windows.

"Nobody here lad, be on your way."

Harry wanted to ask why it was anything to do with the police because he knew exactly what had happened, Mr Fletcher had got drunk in The Greyhound at the bottom of the village, weaved his way all the way up Church Street , collapsed and frozen to death in his stupor where Harry found him. In his mind's eye Harry could still see the single long line of wavering footprints which ended where George's dad lay in the snow. There were no others. The police man looked in no mood to talk though, so he turned away and headed up the narrow lane away from the village. He knew where he needed to be and within five minutes he was leaning on the gate of Captain's field. He would have been sledging down this field later if the night's terrible events hadn't unfolded as they did and he knew that after school lots of children would be making the long steep slope ring with excited squeals and cries as they skimmed down it on their home made toboggans. Harry tried really hard to feel sad but really he felt a mixture of anger that George's father had let his family down so badly by dying and disappointment that he was going to miss the fun the others would have sledging without him. He felt guilty and stood for a while leaning on the gate and trying to cry but it just wouldn't come, there was just a numb feeling in his chest. Captain stood far down the field busy with a pile of hay that old Bemrose had thrown in for him earlier and didn't respond to Harry's calls with more than a toss of his head so he clambered over the gate and headed through the deep snow towards the giant horse. The ground beneath would be way too hard for the farmer to plough so Captain had a day's rest. The snow was powdery and soft and Harry comforted himself with the thought that it was the wrong sort for sledging so he wasn't really going to miss out. In his heart he knew that was wrong but it helped all the same. As he approached, Captain raised his head and nickered, great plumes of steamy breath enveloping his head in the freezing air, then returned to his hay. Harry was close enough to hear the steady grind of his teeth and he was struck by a thought. Why couldn't his life be this simple? Days of work punctuated by quiet contemplation and nothing to worry about but where the next food would come from.

"Hello lad," he said reaching out his hand. The horse shook his head when he felt the hand on his neck startling Harry and making him jump, "You're alright aren't you? You don't ask me questions do you boy?" Before he knew it Harry was leaning against the old horse's shoulder with his face pressed against his broad hot neck, breathing in the sweet sour aroma of sweat and toil, pouring out the story of last night's events. He told him of his fright and horror and his sadness for George and Sarah, how kind Mr Fletcher could be and how he'd saved him from Robert Fox's fists and he told him of his anger that a father could leave his children alone in such a pointless way. George and Sarah would have to live the rest of their lives explaining that their father had died beneath the church wall, frozen to death as a result of drink and that was a terrible, shameful thing. He leaned there thinking perhaps he could have saved him if only he'd remembered that his cornet was missing a little earlier. Then he had a selfish thought that if his father hadn't left it in the first place then someone else would have found the body and he wouldn't be suffering like this with all the questions and curiosity and the horrible picture of Mr Fletcher's grey face, stone eyes and hanging mouth that came every time he closed his eyes. Captain stirred and shifted his enormous weight, swinging his great head round to look at Harry and something in his wise brown eye started Harry's tears at last.

CHAPTER TEN:

Spring 1914

"Do it again Harry, that un's no good, there's a gap in t'corner, tha's not packed it down enough. If we were to use that it'd spit or it might even burst then we've got a problem and somebody'd get hurt. Try again but don't waste t'sand just get a bit more."

Harry sighed and watched Mr Blenkiron's broad back making its way back down the moulding shop to inspect the work of another apprentice. Since finishing school on his fourteenth birthday Harry had been apprenticed at the local steel works, William Green and Co. as a moulder which was one of the most skilled and difficult jobs in the factory. His father had tried to dissuade him from starting work at such a young age wanting Harry to go to Ecclesfield Grammar and get a School Certificate but Harry was adamant that he wanted to work like most of his pals so Mr Jones had put his name forward for an apprenticeship and was proud when Harry was put among the pattern makers and moulders who were some of the most skilful and respected men in the factory. Harry's job was to fill the lower casting box or "flask" where the metal part would be made, with sand then carefully place the carved wooden pattern on top and using a big wooden mallet hammer the pattern into the sand until it was half submerged. He then had to carefully lift the pattern back out, coat the depression it left in the sand with a mixture of finer sand and coal dust then put the pattern back in and hammer again to make the sand solid and ready to receive the molten steel. If he didn't hammer with even pressure the mould would be out of shape and useless and if any sand tumbled back in when he lifted the pattern out it would leave lumps and gaps which would also spoil it and could lead to an explosion of liquid steel. The men made it look easy but Harry spoiled more moulds than he made good ones. Luckily Mr Blenkiron was a patient overseer and provided his boys learnt from the errors they made and improved each time, he was happy.

He didn't see much of his dad because he worked as a fitter at the other end of the factory, building the great ovens and cooking apparatus which was installed in ships being built in Liverpool and Glasgow and Belfast. It made him feel proud though to be doing man's work in the same steel factory where his father, grandfather and all the generations of his family he knew of had worked. It felt almost as if he'd just dropped into a place of work and a way of life that had been quietly waiting for him. Frank started on the same day as Harry but he was destined for another path as his intelligence had been recognised straight away meaning he was set on in the office as a junior clerk. Harry glimpsed him from time to time through the windows of the room above the shop floor that looked down on the men toiling below. He was dressed in a suit and wore a stiff collar and tie. He was always clean and tidy with his hair slicked either side of a centre parting and Harry thought he was having far less fun than he was. He enjoyed the grime and grind and noise of the shop floor, it made him feel manly to look at his calloused, filthy hands at the end of a shift and feel the ache of honest labour in his arms and back.

With a sigh he slid the bottom box out of its frame, tipped the sand back out into the sand box and started the process again. He wasn't going to make the same mistake again so this time he was extra careful to pack the sand tightly into the corners. He knew the mistake he'd made and was a bit cross with himself because it was one of the first things he had been taught; to smooth excess sand away from around the pattern after he'd hammered it in was fundamental to the process and in his rush he had forgotten so he didn't spot the little air pockets that Mr Blenkiron's keen eye had seen. He heaved the wooden pattern onto the middle of the sand and picked up the great mallet he had to use to bash it in. In his first few days it had seemed impossibly heavy and his arms had wobbled and ached every evening as he tried to ease the pain in a hot bath in front of the fire but now he was pleased and proud of the muscles that had started to bulge in his forearms. It helped his playing too and he found he could hold his cornet up for much longer with no discomfort at all. He swung the mallet high and brought it down square and hard on the pattern which sank a few inches into the mould. This time he took his board and carefully scraped away the sand that had been displaced and delivered another mighty bash until only the top inch of the pattern stood proud then he carefully lifted it out to inspect his work. Perfect! He called Mr Blenkiron over to look.

"Nah then Harry, let's have a look see," he said, "aye that's it son, good job, we'll make a moulder of thee yet!" He tousled Harry's hair and walked away to inspect another lad's work calling over his shoulder, "Every time like that now Harry, we've a rush on so no slacking."

At snap time Harry took his sandwich out behind the factory where the stream ran that had once powered the mighty machinery of the forge. The wheel had long since crumbled but its stone housing was still there and a kingfisher had taken to perching on the rough stone wall awaiting the silver flash of sticklebacks to hunt. Harry sat on some tumbled masonry and was soon rewarded with the burst of dazzling turquoise and orange he was hoping for as the little bird skimmed up the stream towards him and landed with a flick of its wings in its usual place. Harry's brawn sandwich was halfway to his mouth and he took a bite then carefully lowered it as he didn't want to startle the bird. Its colours seemed so incongruous after the browns and greys of the workshop where the only brightness was the red and white glow of hot metal and the terrifying fire of the furnaces. Suddenly it dived and in a blink there was a splash, a flurry and it was back on its perch with a wriggling little fish sparking silver and pink in its beak. Harry watched as it juggled the fish around until its head was facing down its throat then it tipped its head back and with a few gulps the creature was gone and the kingfisher turned to wiping its beak sideways against the stone, sharpening for the next hunt. Harry had wondered why the fish had to disappear headfirst and his dad told him it was because the spines on the fish's back lay flat that way round; the other way round they would have lifted up and choked the bird. Harry was transfixed, watching the kingfisher dive over and over again and didn't notice that someone was standing behind him until he heard a sharp twang and an instant later a stone thudded into the kingfisher's perch and the bird flew away.
"I'll have it next time."

Harry jerked round, there was only one person he knew who could have done such a thing.

"What tha looking at? It's vermin, it wants shooting!"

A catapult hung in Foxy's hand, the black rubber band dangling slack now. It was of the kind anglers use to fire bait far out into a pond to attract fish.

"Why? What harm's it done you Foxy?" Harry said.

"It eats babby fish, I've just seen it."

"It was a stickleback and as far as I know fishermen don't usually fish for them because they don't put up much of a fight and they don't taste very good either. Are you stupid or what?"

"Tha what?"

"Well have you seen the size of it? It's only about four inches long! How many fish do you think it can eat? It's hardly going to swallow a pike is it?"

Foxy's mean eyes narrowed.

"Tha'd better not talk to me like that Jonesy, I'll flatten thee and I can get you sacked an'all."

"Oh aye? How're you going to manage that?"

"Well I'm on my dinner, how about you? According to my watch you should have been back ten minutes ago. All I've got to do is report you to Mr Blenkiron and he'll give you your cards." He turned the face of a battered silver pocket watch on a dirty chain towards Harry and grinned.

Although he wasn't particularly scared of Foxy's fists any more Harry could see he was beaten and with a sigh he pushed past him and went back into the gloom, clang and swelter of the shop floor. He cursed his own stupidity; he was so enraptured watching the beautiful little bird that he'd overstepped the strict thirty minutes allowed for lunch and Foxy was right, he could have his apprenticeship taken from him for that. He set straight to work with his head down hoping no one had seen him coming back in and turned over imaginary stories in his head in which he either took terrible, painful revenge on his tormentor or earned his undying gratitude by rescuing him from some outrageous, perilous situation the result of either of which was that at long last Foxy left him alone.

On his way home he met Douglas and Sam who were working the day shift like Harry.

"Summat needs to be done about him," said Douglas when Harry told them what had happened, "why's he have to be so nasty? I don't think he's reight in the head. Who wants to kill a kingfisher?"

"Aye, well we know summat should be done but we've known it since we started little school and we've not come up with a plan yet," said Sam, "he spoils everything and it's all right for you lot, I have to work with him. He's forever calling me names because of my foot but he doesn't do it when t'mesters are listening, he does it quiet like in my ear when I'm working."

"He's a coward like all bullies. I still remember when George's father had hold of him and he wet hisself like a little chabby," Harry added but he felt a twinge of guilt as he said it. There was still a niggle in his head that told him that was because of something unspeakable, some unspoken darkness at the centre of Robert Fox's life that made him the boy he was. Sam looked exhausted, his face was pasty and his limp was very pronounced to the extent that his boot was worn and scuffed where it had been dragging along the ground and when Douglas had gone home Harry asked him if he was all right. "Yes, why?" he said and Harry sensed a prickliness in his voice that suggested this was forbidden territory and he shouldn't be asking. "You just look worn out pal, wondered if it was this business with Foxy"

"I'm knackered Harry, it's this chuffing foot, it's killing me. They've got me fetching and carrying from one end o't'shop to t'other and it's heavy stuff, big lumps o'wood and all sorts and I'm sure they're doing it of a purpose thinking it's a laugh. Foxy's always watching and sniggering. It's giving me some right gyp and I can hardly sleep it hurts that much in t'night."

"Who's your foreman?"

"Mester Jessop but he doesn't do owt in fact I think sometimes it's his idea. He's reight thick wi' Foxy and my pa says he's seen them on a night going in t' White Bear so I'll get nowhere if I complain to him."

"Foxy isn't old enough to go in t'White Bear," Harry exclaimed.

"I know but t'landlord turns a blind eye because Foxy's pa's one of his most loyal customers. He drinks enough ale to keep that place open and I reckon t'landlord's scared of him an'all," Sam replied morosely.

"I can have a word with Mester Blenkiron, see if he can do owt," Harry said, "he's all right is Mester Blenkiron. He helps us and teaches us stuff."

"Not like mine then? I'm supposed to be learning how to be a blacksmith and all I've done so far is fetch and carry and make cups of tea. Don't talk to him Harry, Foxy'll work out it was me that dobbed 'em in and they'll make my life even more of a misery. I shall just have to put up with it. It needs an operation but my mother and father can't afford it so I'm stuck with it."

They were outside Sam's front door and Harry watched sadly as Sam hobbled up the front path between the two beds of brightly coloured summer bulbs, flowers, herbs and vegetables which were flourishing in joyous profusion in the cottage garden. He was struck by how drab and painful Sam's life seemed in contrast. A little broken lad doing man's work and suffering every day. He sighed and felt himself longing for the carefree days of dam building, football and cricket among the cow pats until Robert Fox crept into the edge of his mind's eye to remind him that those times were far from perfect either.

Harry rushed home after calling goodbye to Sam. He had a very important band rehearsal that night as one of the most famous people in the whole brass band community was coming as a guest conductor and he was bringing his son who was reckoned to be one of the finest young cornet players of his generation. The whole family played but Harry Mortimer was turning out to be the star turn and his father Fred wanted to try a new composition out on a band with a soprano cornet player. Harry was bursting with pride that of all the bands in the country, Chapeltown had been chosen. Not only that but in a quiet, private conversation, Norman Barnes had told him that it was because of his growing reputation as one of the most accomplished players of the instrument that Fred and Harry Mortimer were willing to come all the way from Luton where they lived. The piece was called "Mac and Mort" and Mr Barnes said it would be a piece of cake for Harry but he was still nervous and also a little piqued that a young upstart of just twelve years was coming to show them all how it should be done but he'd have to live with that. He flung open the front door expecting to see his dad who usually arrived home from work a little before him but his chair at the table was empty and his mum turned from her work at the big pot sink and said just one word, "Overtime" her eyes were red and her face was a little flushed as if she'd been crying. Harry stopped his onward rush to get ready for band and went over to stand beside her. He was worried because he couldn't remember a time when his mam had been anything other than strong and he'd certainly never seen her cry.

"Are you all right mam?"

"Yes love, just something in my eye, I'll be all right in a minute, must have been a splash of soap or something, you go and get yourself ready"

"Oh, all right," Harry said and he headed for the door that led to the stairs.

"They're saying there's going to be a war."

Her voice was so quiet Harry wasn't quite sure he'd heard it and he had gone through the door before it registered. He turned and went back into the kitchen.

"A war?"

Of course there had been talk among the men at work but he'd only half listened because it had been going on for months and nothing had happened so far but if it had upset his mam then there must have been talk between his parents.

"Aye our Harry a war and a big 'un if nowt's done quick. It's all to do with summat far away on the continent. Nobody I've talked to understands it any better than me but t'papers are full of it, Germans are causing bother and for some reason we have to poke our noses in."

A cold shiver ran down Harry's spine and his stomach lurched. His granddad used to talk about another war that he'd fought in Africa and said it was hell from start to finish. He hadn't been made to go but he'd volunteered for the West Riding Regiment. Harry could remember asking him why he'd joined up and his granddad just said, "Queen and country lad, we can't have flamin' foreigners telling us what to do. We have to defend our Empire." Harry had asked him what it was like because to him it sounded exciting, dressing up in uniform and firing a big gun at the enemy was what every school boy dreamed of doing but his granddad had said, "I saw things no one should ever see Harry. I lost good pals an' all and some o' them that died were bits of lads, still wet behind the ears . They'd seen nowt of life yet and we left them shot and blown to pieces in Africa. No lad it were bloody awful and I hope you never have to see it."

But now his mam was talking about another war that was closer to home.

"Will me dad have to go and fight?" he asked.

"I don't know love, I think it'll just be them in t'army."

"So why are you upset then mam? Surely if they need a lesson teaching we should do it! That's what me dad said at Christmas and all t'lads at work are sayin' t'same."

"They're probably right our Harry, I just get upset when it comes to fighting. That never seems to solve owt."

Harry bristled a little. The men at work, his dad included, had been talking about giving The Kaiser a bashing and they had seemed excited, not upset like his mam though he wasn't entirely sure they'd all grasped that there might be real fighting.

"Go on love, get yourself ready," his mum said, wiping her eyes on the corner of her apron, "it's not for you to worry about it might all just blow over and everyone will come to their senses. Go on, your uniform's set out on t'whatnot, folded up and pressed."

As soon as Harry went out of the room his mam sat heavily down on a kitchen chair. She looked at her hands, red and cracked from work and thought about the day her new husband had slipped a cheap brass band on her finger all those years ago in Ecclesfield church. A gold one had replaced it the following year but the brass one, neatly folded in a handkerchief and kept in a dresser drawer upstairs was the one that meant the most. The thought of losing the loving, gentle man who had given it to her to a war no one seemed to understand was unbearable but try and bear it she must for the sake of her boys. She dabbed her eyes again, carefully rearranged the little posy of spring flowers in a green glass vase on the table, sighed deeply and turned back to her work scrubbing socks in the sink.

It was unheard of for the band to rehearse in their uniform but Mr Barnes was out to impress because it wasn't everyday one of the famous Mortimer family dropped in on a rehearsal. When he announced that full concert uniform was to be worn some of the older men complained because they found it a bit too hot and itchy for the cramped little band room even in winter and this was May and a particularly warm one at that.

"Nay Norman, we'll be boiled in us skins," John-Henry Shaw had said.

"If we are tha'll look like a massive pork sausage John-Henry, thi face goes bright red when tha blowin' at t'best o' times, tha'd better tek it easy tha might pop!"

"Bugger off, Eric, tha no slip of a thing thissen; t'strain on them buttons terrifies me, if one goes when tha playing one of us could lose an eye! I hear tha's got a job being towed about in t'North Atlantic so's t'whalers have got summat to practise their harpoon skills on!"

"Thee shut thi gob John Henry, I've heard tha had a go on t' "speak-your -weight" machine at t'feast and it shouted "One at a time please!"

"All right gentlemen, that'll do, you're both big lads so let's behave like men, not bairns," Norman Barnes said.

"Big?" thought Harry, "enormous more like!" Like many in the brass band world for whom drinking beer was as important as playing John -Henry Shaw and Eric Humberstone both tipped the scales at over twenty stone and their uniforms were stretched tight over enormous bellies. Harry had promised himself he would never become like that, though he did find their verbal sparring and insults quite funny.

He carefully unfolded his uniform from where it sat on a shelf on the whatnot and felt a surge of pride. His mam had pressed knife sharp creases into the trousers and the gold braid and crest sewn onto the jacket shone against the soft, black serge material. He knew the time and effort his mam put into keeping it perfect and as he walked into the kitchen again, his instrument in his hand and his new black lace up boots shone to mirror brightness by his pa, she smiled and nodded. "You look grand our Harry, a proper bobby-dazzler."

"Thanks mam,"

"Get yourself off then and don't be worrying about me, I just get a bit overcome at times, it'll probably all blow over, go on off you pop."

Harry Mortimer turned out to be a quiet, scruffy looking little lad but there was no doubt his playing was at a different level. He soared to the top notes seemingly without effort but could also play at no more than a whisper which was what most impressed Harry. The piece his father had composed was jaunty and fun and the band took to it with relish. Fred Mortimer seemed delighted which was more than could be said for some of the musicians who sweated and shuffled in their scratchy uniforms. When they'd played it a few times Norman Barnes invited him to say a few words and the first thing he said was "There was really no need to dress up lads, you look grand but I don't need that kind of fuss, I'm just a bander like yourselves, so ties and jackets off and let's have you comfortable." There was a mutter of "I telled him there were no need," and "I'm sweating like a beast and all for nowt!" as the men shed layers and stretched.

"I'm very obliged to you men for giving me the chance to hear my little composition and although I say it myself I've not made a bad job; that sounded marvellous. I can go home and tweak it a bit now to make it something decent. Now what did you think to my lad here? He's not bad is he?"

Fishing for compliments was a bit frowned on but there was a general rumble of approval around the room and young Harry Mortimer hissed "Give over father, it's embarrassing" but he raised his hand in acknowledgement. Harry made a beeline for him after they had finished the rehearsal. "Got any tips? You're reight good. I struggle to play quiet like that."

"Yes, have him as your pa!" He pointed to where Fred stood talking to Norman Barnes. "Six hours a day he makes me practice and half of that's just breathing exercises. Try making your embouchure as tight as possible without putting your sop anywhere near and pushing the air out really slowly. I can manage a minute and a half without a new breath. The trick is to keep the flow even and steady. That might help."

"Thanks, I'm going to try that when I get home."

It felt a bit odd asking for advice from such a little lad but Harry was determined to be as good as his namesake so he stuck his hand out to shake. "See you again, happen, you'll be playing t'Albert Hall before too long."

All thoughts of the conversation with his mother were gone when Harry pushed the back door open and shouted "Hello." But he sensed tension in the air and his pa was studying a newspaper with unusual intensity.

"Bobby off and play for an hour," his mother said after he'd told them about the visit from the Mortimers, "me and your father need a talk."

He called for Stan and they came across Frank a little further along the lane playing keepy-uppy. He had the same newspaper in his hand as Harry had seen his father studying. "What's tha reckon to this?" he said, trapping the football beneath his foot and holding the paper out to show them the headline.

"Archduke Ferdinand of Austria Assassinated – Europe on the Brink of War!"

"Who's he when he's at home?" said Stanley.

"No idea but my pa says it's the spark that'll light the powder keg whatever that means," Frank replied. "He reckons all them Austrians and Germans are trying to take over and we might have to fight 'em. He says we can give 'em a bloody nose and put 'em back in their place before it all gets out of hand!"

"Will they come here do you reckon?" Harry said.

"Who?"

"Germans and that."

"They could try, we'd give 'em a reight pasting, they're nowt them! My pa says they're all stupid cowards that sit at home getting fat and eating sausages all day, we'd easy beat 'em in a scrap." He rolled the newspaper into a long thin tube and started bashing Harry about the head with it. "Take THAT and THAT you sausage snaffling cabbage muncher," he yelled before taking off at a gallop towards the cow-field hoofing the ball ahead of him.

All the talk at work the following day was of the news with many of the men excitedly bragging about knocking the Kaiser off his perch or showing the World what English lads were made of. Harry couldn't understand most of it and he suspected he wasn't the only one who had no idea why the killing of an Austrian duke and his wife by some anarchist hundreds of miles away across the sea had anything to do with England's place in the world. He asked Mr Blenkiron when he came to check on his work ; if anyone would know it would be wise, clever Mr Blenkiron, but all he could say was, "Alliances, Harry. We took sides years ago and said we'd fight if anyone on our side was threatened. It seems we're on t'same side as them that killed that archduke and if his lot start a fight we's'll have to join in on t'other side. They're a pompous bloody lot these German types so they could do with a bit of a hiding then we can all get back to normal."

"I thought he was Austrian."

"Same thing lad, Germany, Austria, Hungary, they're all one gang. We've mucked in wi't Frenchies and t'Russians, God knows why and they're in t'opposite team so here we go!"

Harry had seen pictures of Kaiser Wilhelm the leader of Germany in the newspapers and thought he looked stern and unfriendly with his ridiculous moustache that curled half way up his face, not like King George whose large blue eyes sparkled and twinkled when he laughed and whose smile was broad and kind. He had seemed gentle and mild to Harry and he told himself that he was worth fighting for. Excitement like this rarely visited the village and he could almost feel it bubbling.

"Who'll have to fight?'

"We've an army lad, they should see it off pretty sharpish but there's not many of them and they're nearly all abroad so I suppose they'll need some volunteers an'all. I shan't have to do it though, I'm a bit too long in t'tooth."

"I'd love a bash at 'em, who do they think they are?"

Mr Blenkiron smiled and reached out a massive hand to ruffle his hair.

"You're a grand lad Harry but you're a bit young I reckon. By the time you're old enough it'll all be over bar the shouting. Come on, get some work done, you're getting good at it, we'll make a moulder of you yet."

"What about my pa? Could he have a go if it happens?"

"How old is he ?"

Harry had to think, he couldn't remember ever celebrating his father's birthday. He and Laurie always had a smashing day with a present and sometimes even a cake but his mother and father never seemed bothered about their own birthdays. "I think he's about thirty six Mr Blenkiron."

"Probably then but it depends how them in charge set the rules."
"You think it's going to kick off then?"

"Aye, it looks like it. Come on, work now and not so many questions."

CHAPTER ELEVEN:

August 1914

"Are tha coming to t'Newton Hall tomorrow neet? They're signing men up to go and have a bash at 'em. Sooner we get this job done and give old Fritz a bloody nose the better," said Stewart Grange. It was Friday August 7th and England had been officially at war with Germany since Tuesday. The announcement that Germany had invaded Belgium had caused a massive upsurge of patriotic anger and considerable excitement with reports of crowds gathering in the streets of London and stones thrown at the windows of the German Embassy. In Harry's house it was different; his mother had cried and his father had become grim and silent and gone upstairs slamming the bedroom door behind him. Harry, standing in the street listening to his neighbours who had rushed outside at the news, had been swept along by the fervour of it all. Everyone else's father seemed to be there and for the first time in his life Harry had felt a hot flush of shame that his pa wasn't among them. Couldn't he see that the Kaiser needed to be put back in his place, that we had a duty to help the poor little Belgians who were being enslaved by the brutal Hun, that if he wasn't careful he'd miss out on the fun of defeating these stupid fools? Had he forgotten that Harry had met the King? Surely that meant something!

Work had to go on but the excited talk continued when Harry walked into the moulding shop later.

"Nay I don't know, it all feels a bit rushed for my liking, I might wait a bit , see who else fancies it," said George Gregory over his shoulder as he bent over his work filing the rough edges off a casting, stopping now and then to blow the steel dust away and admire his work, "they reckon it'll be a quick do any how so there might not be much point."

"I'd go!" as soon as he'd blurted the words out Harry regretted it."

"You? You little pipsqueak! They don't want kids, they want men!" He could see that George was rattled and he had the uneasy feeling that he'd accidentally challenged his manhood.

"Just saying, if I were old enough I'd volunteer," he mumbled before walking quickly away. His ears felt like they'd burst into flames and he could feel the tears starting.

"Nah then soldier boy, I want hold of you."

Harry felt a hand grab his shoulder and he found himself spun round to face the sneering face of Robert Fox.

"I heard what you said just now Jonesy, I'd watch out if I were you, George Gregory's likely to give you a reight hiding for what you said, especially if I tell him you've been calling him a coward."

"What you on about Foxy? You know I didn't say owt like that !"

"Mebbe I do but he doesn't and I could allus tell him."

"Just leave me alone will you? I've work to do."

"I will leave you alone," Foxy said and to Harry's surprise he released his tight grip allowing Harry to turn his back and begin to walk away but seconds later he felt a tremendous blow to his lower back which sent him sprawling onto the workshop floor. The next thing he knew the bully had straddled him and grabbed a handful of his hair. He leaned down with his face next to Harry's ear and he hissed "for five bob." Harry felt a spray of spittle on his cheek then Mr Blenkiron's voice rang out from further down the shop floor.

"That'll do you boys, play in your own time and not in here!"

"Five bob by tomorrow or I'm telling George Gregory what you called him."

He glanced towards Mr Blenkiron, gave Harry's hair a playful ruffle and stood up. "Only joshin' Mester Blenkiron, sorry!"

"Aye well any more and I'll josh you out of your job Fox!"

"All reight sir, understood, won't happen again sir, he cheeked me that's all and these younger lads need putting in their place from time to time."

"All right lad, less talk and more work."

Foxy walked away and Mr Blenkiron called Harry to him.

"All right Harry? What was that about?"

If there was one thing Harry was not it was a snitch and anyway Robert Fox would wriggle out of any trouble like a fairground greased piglet.

"Nowt, we were just messing and it got a bit out of hand Mr Blenkiron."

The older man looked at Harry long and hard before saying, "Well as long as you're sure," before walking away shaking his head.

Harry bent to his work, the ache of Robert Fox's boot mark made him wince but not as much as the thought of having to hand over five hard earned shillings. He'd keep his stupid trap shut next time.

It came in waves all day, declarations of patriotism, talk of fighting in Africa from the older men, uninformed but passionate denunciations of all things German, sympathy for poor little Belgium, boastful talk of what men would do given a chance and a general feeling that at last the men might be part of something thrilling and glorious, something that would, for however brief a time, lift them from the humdrum banality of their daily lives.

Laurie was sitting on the front step trying to burn paper using a magnifying glass when Harry arrived home. He was happily absorbed and didn't look up when Harry said, "Is Pa home?"

"In t' kitchen, he got in half an hour back. They've been talking!" he added with heavy emphasis. There was no sign of Harry's father when he opened the kitchen door but his mother was arranging a few flowers in a little glass vase humming happily as she did it. "Has Pa gone to t'Newton Hall with all t'others."

"No love, he's not. They've told him at Green's to wait for a bit because they might need men like him to stay in t'works now it's kicked off."

"You mean everybody else's dad'll be going and mine'll be staying at home?" tears began to well in Harry's eyes.

"Looks that way love, yes. Marvellous isn't it?"

"NO! NO it bloody isn't!" Harry shouted. The shame was overwhelming. How could he face his mates? His own father would be labeled a coward.

The smack that hit him hard on the side of his head broke the dam and he began to sob.

"Don't you EVER use language in this house. You might hear it at work but not here my lad," his mother shouted after him as he careered back out into the garden almost flattening Laurie as he barged past him.

"Told you they'd been talking!"

Harry didn't think he'd ever been this miserable, first there was the shame of his pa not joining with the other men and on top of that he had to find five shillings to stop Foxy from bullying him. Five shillings he usually handed over to his mam as soon as he was paid. The worst part was he couldn't share any of this with his mates or indeed anyone. Whatever happened he wouldn't be called a snitch. He headed to Captain's field; the great, gentle horse didn't judge and though he couldn't solve Harry's problems he at least seemed to listen. He was standing in the shade of the chestnut tree which spread its massive boughs across the bottom corner of the long sloping field and he raised his head and nickered in answer to Harry's call. He was about to clamber over the fence when Harry heard Frank shout his name.

"Hey up, hold on!"

Frank was trotting towards him with Douglas at his side and they were clearly excited.

"Have you heard? First lot to join up start training at Redmires on t'moors next week! They're getting uniforms and guns so they must have known it were coming. My pa's reight excited he says he can't wait to have a pop at 'em. They reckon they might get sent to Belgium in about two weeks; I wish I were old enough to go with him I bet it'll be a grand beano!" He paused and looked at Harry, "What's up wi' thee? Tha looks like tha's lost a shillin' and found a tanner!"

Harry felt his insides shrivel like a burst balloon and without thinking he blurted out, "Nowt , it's just they've told my old man he can't go because he has to work in't steel works."

"Well that's not his fault, is it?" Douglas said, diplomatic as always, "If they've said he can't go it's not t'same as him saying he won't go, is it?"

"I suppose so, it's just that he doesn't seem that bothered; in fact, if anything him and me mam seem pleased." He stopped as he began to feel his voice wobble and his friends looked away in embarrassment.

"I'm going," Harry said quickly, "I need a cup of water, I'm parched." He knew the boys could see straight through his stupid excuse but he couldn't face them and he turned quickly and headed home; a place he felt ashamed of all of a sudden.

He woke the following morning with a heavy weight in the pit of his stomach and a sense of dread as he knew that he'd be getting his pay packet today and Foxy would be on him in seconds demanding his five bob. He dressed quickly and trotted to the works ahead of his father. For the first time in his life he didn't want to be seen with him but there was an unexpected shock when he arrived. Robert Fox was nowhere to be seen and he hadn't shown up when the gas hooter sounded for the start of the morning shift. Harry threw himself into his work, hammering and packing sand with a fierce sense of purpose and trying not to catch the eye of anyone on the shop floor, sure that eyes were on him, judging him for his father's failure to join up with the other men.

Foxy didn't appear until dinner time when he crept, snivelling to his work bench. He turned to look at Harry with a haunted expression and Harry was shocked to see his nose was swollen and misshapen, his lip was split and bloody and his right eye was just a slit between puffy purple bruised lids. He caught Harry's open mouthed stare and growled "What tha lookin' at you little squirt, I fell ovver, all reight?" There was menace in his voice so Harry turned quickly away. Unless he'd fallen straight onto his face without putting his hands out to save himself at all, his injuries didn't make any sense and Harry felt sure someone had belted him good and hard in the face. He couldn't help remembering Douglas saying something "needed to be done" to stop his bullying of Sam but though he was tall Douglas was a gentle lad who as far as Harry could remember had never had so much as a playground scrap. He couldn't believe he could possibly be responsible for such nasty injuries. No one went near the bigger boy for the whole day. He seemed diminished and somehow less threatening and Harry sensed that the five bob in his paypacket was safe for the moment. He expected to feel relieved and a bit triumphant but he found to his surprise that the overwhelming feeling was one of sadness which he didn't really understand. But Foxy let him alone.

The days crept by and then suddenly one Thursday morning almost all the men were gone. Only the lads, the older men and Harry's father were left.

"They're at Redmires camp training in hand to hand fighting I'm told Harry lad," Mr Blenkiron told him, "I don't know how we s'll carry on, but we must. T'country needs 'em now. They could be abroad in a week."

Harry had hardly exchanged a word with his pa since the others signed up and his sense of shame burned anew now. "Oh, reight Mr Blenkiron, I'll get on then." He just couldn't think of anything to say and he walked quickly away to the end of the shop floor and began work. He looked across to Foxy's work bench expecting the usual sneering, threatening leer but was amazed to see his bench empty, strewn with tools lying idle and no sign of his tormentor. It was the same for the rest of the week and at the end of his Saturday morning shift Harry plucked up the courage to ask Mr Blenkiron where Robert Fox was.

"I don't know reight, Harry but t'word is he's lied about his age and joined up."

"Why would he do that?" Harry asked, genuinely puzzled. It irked him to think of Foxy doing something that brave when his own father was still at home doing a cushy job.

"I don't know Harry but I reckon I'd rather face five hundred of them Huns than deal with Robert Fox's father. He's allus knocked that lad about since when he were nowt but a chabby and I expect he's had enough and took his chance to get away."

That answered a lot of lingering questions which had hung in Harry's mind like the dirty stain on Foxy's trousers. A bully had spawned a bully, a son had trodden the same mean and cruel path as his father because he needed to exorcise the pain and despair he had been dealt. It made sense but it didn't take away the misery that Foxy had visited on Harry and he felt a glow of anger that he had escaped and headed for the glory of battle with the other brave men. Why should Robert Fox, the bully, the tormenting, snide bully be admired and envied ? It wasn't fair.

CHAPTER TWELVE:

April 1915

It seemed an ordinary morning, dull grey light peeping softly through Harry's bedroom window as the knocker-upper rapped gently with his pole and called "Time 'arry, give us a word!"

"Aye Alf, I'm up and doin'"

He glanced over at Laurie , still sleeping and thought about giving him a shake then thought better of it and tottered over to the wash stand to splash his face with cool water. Work started at six o'clock and it was now fifteen minutes past five. Birdsong was twinkling outside and Harry thought of his band rehearsal later that evening. The band had kept going even though its numbers were reduced and some of the men would never come back now but old Norman had said "When the lads come back they'll need a grand welcome so we keep going down to the last man breathing."

Harry thought that was a bit excessive when he said it in the late summer of '14 but now it didn't seem so far-fetched as telegrams arrived after each big push. All their recent jobs had been gathering at Chapeltown station to play as another group of pals boarded the train at the start of their long journey to France or Belgium. There was almost a holiday atmosphere each time but it was beginning to feel more and more forced as news came back of the terror that awaited them over the Channel. He dressed quickly and sleepily trundled downstairs. His father was already in the kitchen, standing with his back to the door, leaning on the table with a strange hunch to his shoulders, utterly still, staring at something on the table.

"Morning," Harry said.

Silence.

He tried again, he was used to his father's gloominess these days.

"Morning pa."

Silence.

He went to the end of the table and that was when he understood because lying there was a torn envelope, a sheet of paper with a few inky words on it and a white feather.

Harry couldn't speak. What was there to say in the face of such a badge of cowardice. Reserved occupation be damned, the world thought his own father was a coward. While other men were overseas fighting a hideous war in uniform he was skulking at William Green and Co and walking the lanes in civvies and it had been noticed by women and they had damned him and shamed his family forever; it was too much to bear.

The last he heard as he pushed open the door was a great gulping sob and the sound of his father's hard fist slamming down on the table but he didn't care anymore. His hero, his brave pa who flicked molten metal from off his forearms with nothing more than a grunt of irritation was a secret shadow now, a shame like a stain to be hidden and denied. Harry's big heart broke that day and his safe, warm world felt cold and indifferent now. He worked in silence all day, spoke to no one and the elderly men and young lads who were keeping the factory alive sensed that they must not approach him.

He passed The Black Bull on his way home and glimpsed his father already in there, alone, a pint of black porter in his hand and two empty glasses already on the bar beside him. "At least he feels something," Harry thought. He walked up Wheel Lane past Middleton fields and glanced down the slope to the tree where Captain used to seek shade. The horse hadn't been in the field for six months now but Harry couldn't stop himself from looking, "Commandeered for t'war effort 'arry," old farmer Bemrose had said sadly in his strange high pitched, sing song voice, "they need all t'osses and beasts they can get their 'ands on to pull big guns. They say t'mud's terrible." He'd shaken his head and wandered off leaving Harry with just memories of the great animal's comforting presence. He found he could conjour the smell of Captain's flank and the gaze of his kind , brown eye so readily it was almost tangible and too much to bear. The horse had saved him from Foxy's brutal fists once and now he was gone too.

He couldn't eat when he got home and went straight upstairs to take his anger out on his cornet, blasting exercise after exercise out without a mute until his mother hammered on the door and shouted at him to "Shut his racket up"

"It wasn't racket when I played for t'king," he thought but he didn't say anything, just packed the beautiful thing away and lay on his back on the bed staring at the ceiling waiting for rehearsal time, thoughts churning over and over in his mind. On his way, later he met Frank, Stanley and Sam mooching in the lane. "Nah then Harry, all reight old sport?" Frank said

"Not bad, you?"

"As well as can be expected given the trying circumstances of a European war and the fact that me mam's on at me all t'time to be "the man of the house" now my pa's bobbied off to do his bit. What that means my friends is me having to do all t'fetching and carrying, shovelling coal, washing t'pots (and since when were that man's work?) and digging t'bloody garden as well as twelve hour shifts……….. apart from that, champion!" As usual fifty words where one would have done but Harry smiled. At least Frank's father had gone.

"Where is he?" Sam asked.

"Somewhere called Wipers in Belgium apparently. We've only had one letter from him. He's having a grand time, hasn't seen a Fritz yet though. That were six weeks back and we've heard nowt since. I saw in t'paper that it were getting a bit tense and they reckoned summat might kick off soon so he might have a chance at knocking a few over. Wish I were with him, I'd love a pop at old Fritzy boy!"

He mimed holding a Lee Enfield to his shoulder and firing off a round in Sam's direction and Sam pantomimed a dramatic, staggering death shouting guttural sounds that he thought sounded like German might sound before crumpling to the ground with his tongue sticking out of the side of his mouth and his eyes crossed. Harry smiled but he didn't feel like joining in. Since the white feather all the fun had seeped out of him like coloured ink leaving only monochrome in his life.

"So long," he said.

"Wheer tha goin'? Harold me old stick?" Frank said, placing his imaginary rifle in the "shoulder arms" position.

"Band."

"Then be on your way my friend!" and he broke into song, "Don't sigh-ee, don't cry-ee, there's a silver lining in the sky-ee! Bonsoir old thing cheerioh chin chin, Na-poo toodle-oo, goodby-ee!"

"Bye lads," Harry said quietly and there was something in the catch in his voice that hinted at finality as he walked away.

Frank and Sam watched him as he headed towards the village.

"Queer fish that Harry," said Frank quietly. None of them noticed that he turned right towards the village hall instead of left towards the band room when he reached Church Street.

CHAPTER THIRTEEN:

MAY 1915

Harry was bored. It was a hot day and his oversized uniform was itchy and uncomfortable and he was sure there was something crawling about in there. His puttees felt tight and his hair was plastered to his head underneath his tin helmet. Some of the men were asleep on their backs on the duckboards but he was on guard duty doing a four hour watch. He lifted his periscope wearily into his hands and raised it carefully above the trench parapet. Nothing as usual. The barbed wire was intact in front of both trenches, his own and the German trench a hundred yards or so away across the tangled mess of no man's land. The sergeant had said,"If you see even a flicker of movement from old Fritz blast summat out on your bugle, doesn't matter what it is, just make it good and loud, they might be about to pay us a visit and we want to be ready. Be terrible if they got here and we'd not got tea and cakes ready for 'em!"

Harry had grinned and said,

"Tea and cakes and a bloody great knife to cut 'em with," and he'd indicated his bayonet hanging in its "frog" a sort of long leather scabbard with a steel tip which hung from his belt.

"We'll make 'em very welcome eh sir?"

To be honest Harry was horrified by the vicious great knife. During his weeks of training after he'd signed up he'd spent hours running at stuffed sacks hung from a wooden frame, yelling a blood curdling war cry before plunging the bayonet in, twisting it and wrenching it back out. It was fun and manly and playful. This wasn't! The thought of that straw sack being a living breathing man's belly, a man trying to do the same to you didn't bear thinking about, so Harry turned it all into one big joke in his head as did most of the others. He had no idea whether he'd be able to actually do it if the moment came but the more you thought about it the less likely it was. A heavy blanket of avoidance had to be thrown over it in the mind; if it came to it then you just hoped that instinct and self-preservation would kick in.

Signing up had been much quicker and easier than he'd thought on that fateful spring evening. The enormous recruiting sergeant with his great yellow sweeping moustache was sitting alone in the musty village hall with a pile of papers at his elbow. He rose to his feet and towered behind his desk. "Yes sonny? Are you looking for somebody?"

It was now or never.

"I want to join up."

The sergeant looked at him narrowly. "You have to be nineteen lad, you don't look it."

"Well I am, all my family's little, my pa's only five foot three."

"And what use do you think a little 'un like you is going to be, nineteen or not?"

"I can play a bugle, you need them don't you?"

"It's not the nineteenth century lad, we don't gallop about on 'osses blowing fancy tunes any more you know!" the sergeant said, but something was chiming in the back of his head, he'd heard General Sir John French talking at a rally in Leeds a few weeks ago and his speech was all about soldier morale and the need for clear and firm discipline. Perhaps the rousing notes of the bugle ringing out across the battlefield wasn't such a bad idea after all.

"I've got my cornet with me, it's nearly the same if you want to hear," Harry said.

"Go on then, let's hear you," the giant man said, sitting heavily back down. Harry took his precious instrument out and raised it to his lips. He showed the sergeant that he wasn't using the valves and blasted out the reveille followed by the alarm. The noise filled the dusty hall and Harry noticed that the sergeant's eyebrows and moustache wiggled in a gratifying way as he played.

"How old did you say you were son?"

"Nineteen sir," said Harry stoutly

"Date of birth?"

Twelfth of March Eighteen ninety six sir!" The lie slipped smoothly out. It was the first one Harry had ever told but it felt easy and right. Somebody had to step up to the mark and do his bit and if it couldn't be his pa then it had to be him.

The old man stroked his moustache, eying Harry quizzically for what seemed an age then with a sigh he said, "All right lad, you're in," and he pushed a piece of buff coloured paper towards him. "Sign at the bottom."

He pushed an inkwell and pen towards him and taking a deep breath Harry dipped the nib and with a shaking hand signed his name. He took an oath holding a bible and it was over.

"Next room for a medical and if you pass, back here tomorrow for your uniform and orders."

The bored doctor in the next room looked a bit surprised when Harry knocked and walked in but gave him a quick look over, glanced down his throat, checked his feet and said "A1, you'll do. Off you go lad."

As he walked through the door into the sunshine, Harry heard him call, "Good luck son!"

And that was it; he was a bugler in the Army.

It was terrible telling his parents and brother that night and if he allowed himself to think about the tears and shouting and the look of horror on Laurie's face it was almost unbearable. He'd seen it through though and after a few weeks' hard training he found himself on a boat to France, his new, shiny bugle slung on a silken cord round his neck.

"Nah then 'Arry, blow t'mess call, it's time for some delicious bread and jam …..again!"

Harry was jerked back to the present and he turned and grinned at the little corporal who had sneaked up on him. "Right-o Corporal sir!" He counted himself as lucky having Lance Corporal Jimmy Croggan in charge of him and the other eleven men and lads in his section. He was mild mannered most of the time and only fierce when he needed to be unlike some of the other corporals who were vicious, sadistic little tartars who dished out horrible, sometimes cruel punishments for even the slightest misdemeanours. Jimmy was a tiny man with a broad grinning mouth and a spectacular, bristling black moustache like a yard brush. His eyes twinkled constantly and he was a devil for cadging cigarettes and tobacco from his lads.

Harry had lost count of the times he'd had to explain to him that he didn't smoke every time he said, "Gorra fag? Go twos with you?" He'd tried smoking as soon as he arrived at his posting because it seemed to give everyone else so much pleasure and he liked to watch their deft fingers rolling the sweet-smelling tobacco into skinny little cigarettes but it made him cough so violently that he was baffled as to why anyone would do it because it felt like torture to him. His eyes had watered and he'd felt sick for half an hour afterwards much to the amusement of the other men who all seemed to be seasoned smokers.

He raised his bugle and played the Mess Call and men began to appear from dugouts and bends in the trench, heading for the communication trench to take them back to where a harassed cook was slapping margarine and plum and apple jam on badly cut lumps of greyish bread.

"Keep your ead's down lads we don't want anybody getting a new hair parting do we? If you've used your tin 'at to sup soup out of now's the time to empty it out and pop it on your noggin," Corporal Croggan shouted as they scuttled past him. Harry watched them go, stooping almost double like little hunchbacks, swearing and laughing as they went. Not for the first time he reflected how normal this all seemed now. It was almost as if home could only exist if he was actually there, that people were waiting, still and silent in darkness and suspended animation for him to return so they could come to life and go about their daily business. The last of the men passed him and he was left alone; food would come later for him, he still had a couple of hours left on duty. He raised his periscope to peer over the parapet again. Still no movement from the trenches opposite. Poppies and cornflowers were blooming in the broken, pale brown earth of no man's land, ice and fire nodding gently in the hot breeze and above, the tiny dot of a lark trilled and warbled from on high. Harry lowered his periscope and raised himself up a little to gaze upwards towards it. The air suddenly moved just beside his ear and there was a loud thud in the trench wall behind him followed almost instantly by a sharp crack. Puzzled, Harry turned to look stupidly at the mud wall behind him, his mouth open in astonishment. The mud had a hole in it and the edges of the hole were fizzing and bubbling slightly where the hot bullet from the German sniper's rifle had buried itself. The shock took a moment to register then he sank to a sitting position on the duckboards and began to tremble violently. What had seemed like a boring game had snapped into horrible reality; that was how easy it was to die here. One moment's lapse in attention had nearly cost him his life. The enemy were no longer vague grey shapes momentarily glimpsed in the far distance, shimmering in the heat but real living men with guns in their hands that were trying to kill him. He looked at his own shaking musician's hands. Would they be capable of doing the same if it came to it?

"What's up lad? You look as if you've had some bad news!"

Harry stared at Corporal Croggan but no words would come.

"Have you nearly bought one son? Has old Fritz had a go at you with his little pop gun?"

Harry nodded dumbly.

"Happened to me early on and I'll tell you what, you'll not do it again! Go on, bugger off and get a bit of snap and a cup of tea down you, I'll look after your watch for a bit. You're white as a sheet! Go on, and keep your chuffin' 'ead down." He reached out and rapped on Harry's tin helmet. "We want you in one piece lad, else who'll keep us in order with that bugle of yours?" He smiled and twitched his moustache giving Harry a big wink before pushing him gently in the direction of the communication trench the other men had used. Harry hauled himself onto India rubber legs and began to make his way. Half way there he was sick but he forced himself onward until the mess sergeant shoved a lump of bread smeared with sticky, brownish jam into one hand and a tin mug of boiling tea into the other. "You've two minutes before t'next lot come and I'll be needing that mug so get a shift on," the sergeant grunted at him. He'd seen shaky white-faced soldiers before and knew that a hot jolt of tea normally put them right after a scare. He thought this lad looked too young to have gone for a soldier, with his too big uniform and smooth chin but who was he to say?

Harry took a gulp, wincing as the hot tea scalded his gullet on its way down. Everyone else seemed happy, laughing and joshing with each other as they crammed the bread into their mouths. Amongst the faces Harry suddenly realised one was familiar. John Fenwick was standing drinking tea with a group of other Tommies. He looked older and much more tired than Harry remembered him but it was definitely him; he even still had the slight depression in his top lip caused by years of playing a brass instrument. He caught Harry's eye just as Harry caught his and smiled uncertainly. He sauntered over.

"Is it 'Arry?"

"Hello John, all reight?"

"Aye, in the pink, we've got it cushy here so far. When did you get here? I thought you'd still be back in good old Blighty knocking tunes out with old Norman. Bit young for this lark aren't you?"

"You could say that, but you're t'same. You're a bit too young an'all aren't you?" Harry said, a bit stung by John's question.

"I was when I joined up wi' t'pals battalion in '14; I was eighteen then so I could be in t'army at home but they couldn't send me over here until my nineteenth birthday. I got my orders on the day after I turned nineteen and I've been here ever since and so far nowt much has happened in this section. Looks like they're sending any bugger over now then! How old are you Harry?" He paused looking keenly at Harry's face. "Tha looks a bit pasty old stick, has summat happened? Here sit down for a bit, I'll hold your tea," and he took the slopping cup from Harry's hand and held his elbow while he sat gingerly down on the dusty ground. John squatted beside him, a look of sincere concern on his freckled face.

"I nearly copped a packet just now," Harry said trying hard to control the wobble in his voice and be the man he clearly wasn't, "Boche sniper nearly had me up the line."

"A what ?"

"Sniper, you know a crackshot, I got my head a bit too high and next thing I know there's a whizz and a crack and a big bullet hole in t'trench wall an inch to t'left of me left ear."

"Good job it weren't an inch to t'right," John said, grinning.

"Why?" Harry said, puzzled by the smile.

"Because an inch to t'right'd be smack in t'middle of your forehead!"

"Oh aye! Flipping hilarious," Harry said in a peevish tone.

"Oh come on Harry, you've got to laugh or else you'd cry! You've had a lucky one, old Fritz missed you and you've learnt your lesson, I'm guessing you'll not be offering your napper for target practise again any time in the near future?" he paused, waiting until a wan smile began to appear on Harry's white face. "What have they had you doing so far soldier boy?"

"Guard duty mainly and a bit of bugling every now and then but they've told me that might have to stop up here at the line because it's giving too much away to Fritz, telling him what we're up to. I did loads of it back behind the line in rest camp before they sent me forward so I expect that'll start again when we get stood down."

"I wondered who it were disturbing my beauty sleep every morning making that horrible racket, I never imagined it'd be a Chapeltown bandsman!"

"Well I didn't really expect to be here either but ……" He trailed off; he couldn't tell John the real reason it was just too shameful. "I just fancied it," he added weakly.

"Aye, I suppose I were t'same," John said, "not so sure now though. I thought we'd be doing some proper fighting but all we've done is sup tea and dig bloomin' trenches I've never been so bored in my life. I'd have been better off at 'ome; at least I were doin' something useful. Only thing that's good about it is I've met some grand chaps and I don't have to listen to me mam nagging on!"

Harry would have given a gold pig to have his mam nagging on but he just nodded dumbly and sipped his scalding tea.

"Any road young 'un I've to get back, happen I'll see you around and for God's sake keep yer flippin' 'ead down!"

He sauntered back to his pals and Harry watched as they crouched and began to make their way back along the narrow communication trench in single file like a khaki coloured centipede.

The tea had worked its magic and Harry felt restored at least physically so he popped his tin mug back on the field table behind which the enormous mess sergeant stood like a great angry pop eyed walrus and began to make his way back to where Corporal Croggan was waiting. At least now he had a story to tell the other lads in the platoon though he resolved in his head not to mention it in his next letter home. Somehow escaping death so narrowly made him feel more of a man but he still missed his mam and Laurie and when he imagined them receiving a telegram telling them he had been killed in action he felt a great well of sorrow and sadness beginning to form inside him like a cloud of black ink in a pool. Corporal Croggan was waiting patiently sitting on the fire step when Harry got back a few minutes later, "Nah then! Fancy you two having the same name!" he said taking a draw on a spindly rolled up gasper and blowing the smoke in two plumes from his nostrils like a little moustachioed dragon.

"Which two? What you on about Corp?" asked Harry, baffled.

"You and Houdini, both called Harry; both narrowly escape certain death!"

"Oh aye, very funny Corp!" said Harry with heavy sarcasm.

The nickname stuck and Harry soon took to it. It made him different and he could think of much worse Music Hall acts to be named after, Little Titch would have been more appropriate, but Houdini he became.

The days dragged by and still nothing happened. The weather remained hot and the men spent sultry, sweaty days complaining about the lack of action, the scratch and tickle of their uniforms, the endless, seemingly pointless drills where they were screamed at by Sergeant Major Blackwell and more than anything else the boredom. They filled their time playing cards, cutting each other's hair, cleaning kit and chasing the lice, which infested all their uniforms, along the seams with a lighted Lucifer grunting with satisfaction when they heard them crackle and pop in the flame. One day there was great excitement because a sack of mail from home arrived and nearly all the men received a letter. Harry's was in three parts, a page from his mam, one from Laurie and another in his Pa's cramped spidery hand. He crept into a small dugout in the trench wall and began to read. His Ma's letter was full of concern about whether he was being treated well, how much he was getting to eat, if he had enough socks and a whole paragraph begging him to tell someone the truth about his age and get sent home. Laurie's was a mixture of badly spelt jokes and tales of school and the fun he was having with his pals around the fields and village which made Harry's heart ache for that life which seemed so far away from him now even though in reality it was only a couple of years since he and his mates had been dam building at Wood End. He felt the scar on his head and smiled. So far messing about building a dam in a stream with his mates had proved more painful than being at war. Laurie's letter ended with a cheery "Good-byee" which made Harry smile, he must have been to Attercliffe Palace Music Hall and seen Harry Tate who'd made it his catch phrase. It was strange to think that while he was sitting in a muddy hole in the side of a trench other people were laughing at a comedian in a theatre. With a jolt he suddenly realised why Laurie had been given such a treat, it was exactly two weeks since his birthday. He fought back the tears and picked up his Pa's letter. To his amazement it was full of pride and praise, telling Harry that he had done the right thing and been a true British man in his country's hour of need. He ended by saying he would be there with him if it weren't for the "Bloody Government" needing him in his reserved occupation. Harry felt angry. Why hadn't his pa talked properly to him? Why had he let the whole village believe he was a coward resulting in the terrible white feather? Why hadn't he stood up for himself? The questions burned but didn't help because there were no answers but after a few moments he began to feel a little better about his father, perhaps it was really the fault of "The bloody government" after all and at least he'd made him proud.

It was quiet in the trench while the men read their mail, punctuated by the odd muffled sob or guffaw of laughter dependent on what the crumpled little sheets of paper contained but at least it was something to do compared to the usual stultifying boredom of trench life. Harry folded the sheets of paper and tucked them into the top pocket of his battle blouse. He'd read it again later and see if it made him feel the same way about his pa. He was sitting staring into space, thinking when a figure suddenly appeared in front of him and blocked out the sun . He squinted but couldn't make out a face as the person was silhouetted and unmoving. Harry's heart raced, was it the Sarge? Had he missed a duty? Was he supposed to be stood to? He couldn't think of anything he'd failed to do and besides this man seemed too thin to be the Sergeant Blackwell and too tall to be corporal Croggan. Harry scrambled to his feet and saluted smartly fearing it might be an even more superior officer, one of the young, godlike men who spoke in voices so refined he could hardly understand them, but found himself looking straight into the deep set, slightly squinting dark eyes of an all too familiar face.

"Well, fancy meeting you here, laddy-lass, I thought you'd be too yitten for t'big picnic!"

"Nah then, Foxy.." but he got no further before he felt a stinging blow on the side of his head.

"Lance-Corporal Fox now you weedy little get and don't you forget it!" Foxy's face was inches from his and Harry could see the spittle gathered at the corners of his mouth and smell the onions the older boy had been eating. His eyes were narrowed, glittering like obsidian and Harry could see his own pale face reflected in them. "I've just been promoted and sent here to make your life a misery Jonesy," he said, his lip curling into a crocodile's smile, "So tha'd better start now, t'latrine trench needs digging deeper, get your shovel and get on with it!"

Something wasn't right, unless Corporal Croggan had been relieved of his duties, Robert Fox couldn't possibly be his Lance Corporal. Each section of a platoon only had one and Foxy wasn't his.

"You're not my Corp, I take my orders from Corporal Croggan," he said, rubbing his red, throbbing ear which was burning like fire from the vicious blow. Foxy hawked up and spat revoltingly on Harry's boot, "You take your orders from any superior officer who happens to dish 'em out or else face a court marshal and probable firing squad and that'd make two cowards in your family so I'd do as I was ordered if I were you."

Then he reached out and ruffled Harry's hair "Oh I'm going to have some fun with you laddy-lass!"

Harry jerked away, the condescension in Foxy's nasal voice was worse than the physical violence. With a sigh he picked up his pack, straightened his puttees, detached his entrenching tool from its loop and said, "Yes Lance-corporal." He tried to get the same level of disdain in his voice that Foxy had used but it didn't work, he just sounded mardy. With a sigh he set off in the direction of the stinking latrine trench but as he approached a bend in the trench he almost bumped into Corporal Croggan coming the other way. "Hey up Houdini, where you heading?"

"Latrine duty Corporal,"

Croggan's eyebrows shot up like two startled mice, "On whose orders?"

"Lance-Corporal Fox sir,' said Harry miserably.

"Who the blue blazes is Lance-Corporal Fox and why is he dishing out orders in my section?"

"He's from my village sir and he says he's been stationed near us." Harry nearly blurted out that Foxy was a mean bully who had made his life a misery back in Blighty but he realised just in time that this kind of complaint would be useless in the trenches. Home life had no bearing on what happened here.

"Right Houdini, you're relieved of that duty on my orders and I shall be having a word with this Lance-Corporal Fox," Harry could tell Croggan was rattled but he cut in quickly, "Oh it's all right Corp, just leave him, I think he was just joshing with me." The last thing Harry wanted was Foxy thinking he was a snitch as he'd make his life an absolute misery. The little corporal stiffened, pulled himself up to his full five feet three and fixed Harry with a glare, "I don't need you to give me advice about what I should and shouldn't do bugle boy but I shall be watching this Fox character and if he steps on my toes again I shall be 'avin' words!" He pushed past Harry and began barking orders at a group of men lounging, smoking at the end of the trench, "Brown! Ridge! Lodge! Your watch! Look sharp and don't get your 'eads shot off!"

Two days passed and Harry only glimpsed Foxy in the distance on one occasion when he seemed to be getting a bit of a dressing down from an officer. Perhaps the brass were onto his bullying and he was being told to amend his ways. It was only a guess but it made Harry feel a little better.

In the afternoon corporal Croggan collected his platoon together.

"That's us done for a spell lads, we're being stood down for a week, back behind the lines so gather your kit. We'll be transferring at sixteen hundred hours so be here on the dot or I'll have you on a fizzer!"

A great cheer went up from the little huddle of men and glancing down the trench, Harry could see that the same message was being relayed to other sections of the platoon and a wave of cheers followed each announcement. He glanced at Corporal Croggan who was now in deep conversation a few yards away with Sergeant Blackwell and his face was creased into a serious frown. As Harry watched, the sergeant unfolded a map from his pack and he and Croggan pored over it with Blackwell prodding it occasionally before looking up and pointing at the distant landscape beyond no-man's land. Something was different but Harry couldn't put his finger on it and anyway it wasn't his business. Croggan waved him over, "Nah then Houdini, where's thi trumpet?"

Harry reached behind him and swung the bugle, which hung on its silken cord round in front of him.

"Let's give Fritz summat to talk about, let him know we're a happy bunch. Just before we stand down I want you to blast away so t'lads can sing on their way!"

"Yes Corporal Croggan, I'll do my best," Harry said. It wasn't an easy task as the bugle had no valves and the notes had to be created purely by varying the airflow and adjusting the embouchure which was all well and good for the repertoire of bugle calls but trying to knock out popular songs in a key the lads could sing in without any opportunity to practise was tricky to say the very least. Still he'd give it his best shot! He decided on "Pack up your troubles" as it had a fairly simple tune but was jaunty and popular with the men. He imagined the mouth shapes he'd make and ached for those hours he'd spent in his room doing exercise after exercise and scale after scale until his cheeks hurt and his lip was bruised and swollen. At the time he'd resented it, especially when he could hear other lads playing outside in the spring sunshine but now it seemed like paradise compared to his life now. He imagined his little soprano cornet lying silent and safe in its velvet cocoon in his bedroom at home like a jewel in a dark deep mine and wished he could change places with it.

For the rest of the afternoon he practised with a pair of socks stuffed into his bugle and though it wasn't perfect by any standard he felt he could do a reasonable job.

Fifteen minutes before four found the platoon huddled, slightly crouched at the mouth of the communication trench and on a signal Harry, at the head of the group of men, put his bugle to his lips and began to blast the tune out as loud as he could. The men began to sing lustily and the whole column began to move. There was the immediate crack of rifle fire as the Germans expressed their disapproval but the bullets whined harmlessly overhead as the men kept their heads well below the parapet. Corporal Croggan's face was creased into a wide grin and he trotted up beside Harry and said, "That'll give the buggers summat to wonder about!"

Half way along the communication trench the platoon saw their replacements heading up to the line in a parallel trench fifty yards to their right. They were a young bunch and Harry could tell by their pale faces that this was their first time. He'd felt the same apprehension himself only to find it overcome by the numbing boredom and discomfort of trench life. Waves were exchanged between the two groups of soldiers then they were gone as they were ordered to bend low to avoid sniper fire.

A lowering dark grey sky hung over the men by the time they had trudged the length of the communication trench to the reserve position and just as they were dumping their packs, scratching and stretching and scouting round for somewhere to settle down for the night the order came that they were to move again, further back from the line to a farm where they could rest properly undercover. A subdued cheer went up for though it was a good mile further to walk it was also a mile further away from German sniper fire. Wearily the men hefted their packs back onto their shoulders and began to struggle away over the ploughed ground towards Le Rutoire Farm. "Harry lad!" came a shout, "give 'em summat to march to! And make it lively, they're about done in!"

Harry was exhausted too but an order was an order so he fished out his bugle and began to play an old favourite; "It's a Long Way to Tipperary." Half the lads had no idea what or where Tipperary was but they joined in with gusto and the yards began to swing by beneath their trudging boots. A hundred yards from the low-lying buildings of the farm a dull, repetitive, metallic clanking sound reached them along with the shouts of men and the snorts and stampings of great horses and from behind a stand of oak trees appeared an extraordinary sight. Six heavy horses emerged, steaming at the nostrils, flecked with white salty sweat around their great leather collars and straining against their traces as they hauled enormous guns, each mounted on iron wheels and each with a kind of shield of metal through which poked a ten foot long barrel. Harry's heart lurched as the mighty animals plodded towards them. Surely that massive chestnut was Captain, his old friend and protector from Middleton fields. Of course a closer look told him immediately that it wasn't and he felt a little foolish for even thinking such an outlandish coincidence could be possible but it made his heart ache for those days leaning against his giant flank in the warm sunshine breathing in his deep, comforting smell and stroking his dappled shoulder.

Corporal Croggan called, "Right lads this is home for a few days, so set to and find a billet. T'farmer's been gone a while, apparently he reckoned old Fritz was a bit too close for comfort and he scarpered so it's all ours."

Harry headed towards a barn watching the rolling guns as he went. He and the others who came with him struck lucky as the barn had a thick layer of hay over the beaten earth floor as well as a sloping heap in one corner. Within minutes the men had thrown off their packs, made nests in the hay and were lying, stretched out, luxuriating and sharing jokes. Harry headed for the great heap in the corner and threw himself down only to leap back to his feet as a rat squirmed out from beneath his back causing him to cry out in alarm. "What's up Houdini?" one of the men shouted. "Rat!" Harry called back.

"No need to get personal, I only asked what was up," the man shouted, winking at the other lads around him.

"I meant it was a rat that made me jump, I wasn't calling you a …"

Harry's voice trailed off as he realised he'd been had. He had a lot to learn.

"Get yourself bedded down, young 'un I'm only having you on," said the man holding his hand out for Harry to shake. He'd had Harry on a few times since he'd joined the platoon and Harry never quite knew when he was kidding him on. He was a typical dry Yorkshireman who smiled rarely but winked often. "I know you are," he said defensively but settling down beside him. His name was Sam Evans and he was a good twenty years older than Harry and though he was constantly trying to catch him out with silly jokes and tricks he looked out for him without Harry being aware of it.

"Fag?" he said, holding out a crumpled pack.

"No ta, I don't smoke them," Harry said, "and anyway this place is as dry as tinder, if you drop some ash it'll go up like Guy Fawkes Night and we'll all be burned alive."

"Aye Houdini, you're not wrong, I'd better go outside then, coming?"

Out in the still dusk of the warm early evening there was feverish activity as the great guns, along with a dozen more which had now arrived were being dug in and set up a few hundred yards forward of the farm . "Let's go and have a look," Sam said, "I've never been this close to 'em before, just heard 'em in the distance further along the line."

By the time they got there the battery of guns had been positioned in a long straight line across the field, facing the direction Harry's platoon had just come from. Some gunners were looking closely at charts and maps whilst others were adjusting the barrels of the guns by whirling wheels round and round and peering at a spirit level bubble built into the side of the gun-sight. Eventually all the barrels were exactly level, pointing straight ahead parallel to the ground. "I don't get it," Harry said, "if they fire them the shell will just go straight ahead and hit those trees!" But he'd spoken too soon. An order was shouted by an officer peering intently at a chart and the men manning the gun in the centre of the line began to whirl their wheels looking all the time at a device on the gun sight that reminded Harry of the protractor he'd used at school to wrestle with trigonometry problems in Mr Roebuck's sleepy classroom. Gradually the barrel of the gun rose into the air and when the correct angle had been reached the others along the line followed suit. In the gathering dusk they were an awe- inspiring sight, deadly and strangely beautiful at the same time. "Old Fritz is going to cop it when those devils get firing," said Sam, winking at Harry and Harry smiled back. Sam seemed incapable of saying anything without an accompanying wink which was one of the reasons it was so difficult to tell when he was joshing.

As they turned to return to the barn they saw a little figure approaching and he didn't look happy. "Oy! Houdini! Where the bleedin' 'ell have you been? You should have blown "Officers' dinner call" five chuffin' minutes ago ! You'd better do it quick else Sarge will have you on a fizzer for the rest of your life!"

Harry's heart pounded, he'd got so used to being told he mustn't play the usual calls in the front line he'd forgotten it was expected of him behind the line. "Sorry Corporal Croggan, I'll do it right away."

"You'd better put your escape skills into action Houdini," Sam winked, "I'd pay money to see you try and escape jankers ! An officer doesn't like to be kept waiting for his bully beef!"

But Harry didn't escape punishment and the next day found him peeling a huge mound of potatoes that the men had grubbed up from one of the farm's muddy abandoned fields and though it was tedious work that made Harry's hands red raw as he scraped he didn't mind it too much as it allowed him to daydream of home. Into his mind floated his friends, Stanley, Frank, Sam with his "funny" foot, gentle, clever Douglas and poor George, his best ever mate. He wondered what they were all doing now. It was strange to think that even though they were all working they might still be gathering in the cow field for a game of football of a summer's evening except for George of course and who knew what sort of a life he'd had since his father died. Then there was old Norman Barnes and the Chapeltown band. Were they still going? Who was in his chair? Were the Whit Marches happening this year? He resolved to ask all these questions in his next letter home but for now he'd about three hundred potatoes to peel. Just as he reached out to pick one up he was nearly shocked out of his skin by a deafening roar as the great guns opened up and sent their first deadly load screaming into the air. Though they were a good few hundred yards away the stench of cordite soon drifted back to where Harry sat, open mouthed and with ringing ears. He'd never heard a louder or more awe- inspiring noise. Men came running from all areas of the farm to watch, listen and marvel and when the booming stopped after a few minutes, one of Harry's platoon, Eric Ridge turned to him and said, "Just getting range, that'll kick things off now. Fritz'll not be happy! We might actually get to see some action at last. I bet the lads at the front got a shock when that lot came screeching over!"

Harry's first thought though was that if the British guns could reach the German line then surely the German guns could reach them. "No need to worry Houdini," Eric told him, "they don't know we're here behind the guns, they'll be aiming their Howitzers at our trenches and artillery, trying to knock 'em out. It'll be noisy but we're far enough back not to get hit so long as they don't know we're here. There's some men been detailed to watch out for aeroplanes coming over to spy. If that happens we're in a pickle but for now we're safe as houses."

Harry couldn't help thinking that that was very optimistic, but what would he know? He was a fifteen year old bugler from Grenoside, an apprentice moulder with no military experience. Some of these men had fought in the African war and were wily, battle hardened men, though they were in the minority as most of Harry's platoon were young men between the ages of about nineteen and twenty two.

Harry gazed at the smoking guns, the tough men in their vests and braces who were operating them, fags dangling from the corners of their mouths and eyes narrowed against the cordite laden smoke and the wagons loaded with gleaming golden shells glowing in the morning sun. Each gun had a great tub of grease beside it and men were smearing big dollops of it over the moving parts . It would become routine and ordinary over the next few weeks but for now it was novel and exciting; a welcome distraction from the daily grind.

"I say bugler, those spuds aren't going to peel themselves y'know, best get back to the jolly old task in hand, what?"

"Yes sir, right away sir!" Harry said, jerking to attention and saluting smartly. He'd never been spoken to directly by an officer and even though it was a mild reprimand he glowed with pride. The young lieutenant with his neatly clipped moustache and immaculate uniform gave him a smile and turned to go. He'd gone a few yards when he turned around, saluted to Harry and said, "Well done lad, carry on, you're the right sort."

Harry scraped potatoes with renewed vigour for the rest of the afternoon, suffused with a warm glow that made him blush to his collar each time he thought about it, "the right sort!" from an officer, he could hardly believe it.

That evening a rumbling convoy of trucks arrived from the remains of the nearby village of Neuve Chappelle which had seen heavy fighting in the March before Harry joined up in May. They were full of equipment to set up a field kitchen and mess hall in the barns and outbuildings of the farm and also hundreds of low bunks which were set out in serried ranks in an enormous shed which stood alone on the boundary of a field a little way from the farm.

"Well this'll be cushy, we might get some decent kip! Top hole I call it," John-Willy Sprake said as he watched the thin mattresses being placed on the beds.

"You can have one if you want one mate as long as you don't mind having a leg or an arm off or your bollocks shot away, these are for the wounded when the fighting starts. This is a field dressing station from now on. Best bit is they'll be sending some pretty nurses to keep us all happy," grinned the young Sergeant in charge of the operation.

"Oh, reight!" John –Willy said, "I thought it were too good to be true."

"Not be long now then," Sam said "looks like the brasshats are gearing up to let us have a crack at the old square heads, first the guns and now a dressing station. We'll be up and down from the line like a frog up a pump, you just watch!"

But nothing happened.

CHAPTER FOURTEEN:

Early August 1915

The first nurses arrived at the farm at the beginning of August after Harry's company had done two more stints in the line and Harry had never seen men act so daft. They peered into trenching tools polished for make shift mirrors, shaved their faces raw, scrubbed their grubby hands and polished their boots until they could see their faces in them. Moustaches were clipped and hair was trimmed and parted and greased down and some men even tried to iron their uniforms using flat irons they'd found in the old farm kitchen and heated on the company's blacksmith's forge. It was all to no avail as the women were billeted well away from the men's quarters and were only rarely glimpsed going to and fro as they prepared the field hospital but it was enough to know they were there and there was excitement in the air as a concert party had been assembled and there was to be a grand entertainment to which the nurses were to be invited. There was no ill intent or lasciviousness among the men just an aching need to spend time being civilised with female company that reminded them of sweethearts and wives, mothers and sisters back in Blighty. Life among men at the front was rough and often vulgar, jokes were crude and language was fruity to say the least. Having to mind your Ps and Qs for a while and be courteous and gentlemanly brought a whiff of the perfume of home and made the men feel there was a purpose to the war which was difficult to grasp when you were sitting in a muddy hole bored out of your mind with a group of similarly sweaty, stinking, irritable men.

A choir had been assembled and had practised a selection of popular songs every evening for a week. They had begun to sound pleasant and harmonious and Harry had to admit to himself that he'd shed a few tears listening to some of the more poignant songs. "There's a Long, Long Trail A-Winding" with it's beautiful melody and promise of future happiness got him every time. A battered cornet was procured from somewhere and Harry spent happy hours taking it to pieces, cleaning and reassembling it and re-springing the valves with springs made by the company blacksmith until it played reasonably well. Harry loved watching the blacksmith at work because it reminded him of his pa. The same leather apron, the same smell of sizzling burnt hair when sparks flew and the same ability to make something tiny and delicate with massive brawny hands. The ancient cornet buzzed a bit as the bell had worn so thin it had lacy holes in it but it was better than nothing and the men had gathered round, slack jawed in amazement as Harry played a selection of both popular and classical pieces. They roared their approval when he trotted out The Carnival of Venice by the American Herbert Clarke which required a good deal of impressive triple tonguing and clapped and stamped and sang along to "Here we are, Here we are, Here we are again!"

Sam told him, "You shouldn't be messing about out here Harry lad, you should be on t'halls you'd make a packet! When t'fighting starts, cop for a blighty, just a little 'un, a toe or summat and get thissen off home! You're wasted here, a little toe'd be a small price to pay. Might be a bit difficult to organise like, we'd have to paint a target on it and hold you upside down so you could poke your foot over t'parapet. We'd soon see how good a shot old Fritzy boy is!"

"Well he missed me head so I'd surprised if he could hit me toe," Harry said, joining in the joke for once.

"I'm not codding, I mean it," the older man said, his face a mask of seriousness.

"Oh, sorry, it's just it seemed so daft," Harry said, worried he'd offended him.

Sam turned to the men around and winked a slow, deliberate wink. "He's so easy, so very easy!" he said. "Of course I'm joshing, soft lad! As if we'd do that. Take a stronger man than me to go near your feet after a month in the same socks in any case!" he said wafting his hand in front of his nose.

Suddenly Sam's jaw dropped and he stared at something over Harry's shoulder. There was a great shout of laughter from the men and a cacophony of whistles and turning around Harry saw three astoundingly ugly women sashaying across the dusty ground where the men usually gathered to play football. They were dressed in lurid, bright dresses, outlandish bonnets and each twirled a paper parasol over her shoulder. Two of them sported luxuriant moustaches and their army regulation boots peeped out from beneath their skirts as they trotted, twinkle toed in front of the crowd of baying, hooting soldiers. They stopped, faced the men and began to sing in ridiculous, high pitched voices. "She's only a bird in a gilded cage, a beautiful sight to see, you may think she's happy and free from care, she's not though she seems to be!"

Amid the cat -calls and whistles Harry found himself transported back to a sun filled field on the edge of a wood where a yellowhammer called and his daft mate Frank sang back to it in a silly voice.

"To see the rest you cheeky fellows, you'll have to come to the show, we three little maids are off for our beauty sleep now, you can have too much of a good thing you know," said the tallest of the three grotesque figures in the deepest voice he could muster and the three men curtsied elaborately, hitched their dresses up and walked off with a manly swagger towards a tent pitched on the edge of the field.

"Daft buggers," Sam said, turning to Harry, "are you all right son?"

Harry's cheeks were wet and he seemed to be transfixed, his eyes focused elsewhere. Sam's kindly voice brought him back.

"Yes, aye, I'm grand, laughed so much it brought tears to my eyes," he said quickly, turning his face away and wiping his snotty nose on his sleeve. Sam sensed the lie but said nothing, resolving to keep a special eye out for Harry. He was just a lad, this was hard.

August 15th 1915

Dear Mam, Pa and our Laurie

Here we are, here we are, here we are again!

I'm writing this from my comfortable billet in a farm back of the lines again . I can't tell you where we are but it is grand and cushy and we are in great spirits. We had an entertainment last night which was splendid fun! All the birds were in gay mood and some made silly fools of themselves because we had many VAD nurses in the audience. They showed off and stared and puffed themselves up like silly bantam cocks. Of course I didn't, all I could think of when I saw those ladies was you my dearest mama. How I miss you. We had singing from a choir, a good tenor who did songs from two chaps called Gilbert and Sullivan who I gather were all the rage in London in the seventies. Did you ever hear of them? I hadn't but their songs were absolutely spiffing; SO funny. I'm not sure the brass were too thrilled though because they were a bit rude about generals and the like! One of the nurses played some Chopin on the piano (rather badly!) but she still got a huge cheer from the men (I wonder why!!!). Then three chaps came on dressed as ladies and sang some comic songs. I thought I might die laughing! They'd been given special permission not to shave for three days and wore their boots on clear view so it was even funnier. I went last, playing an old battered Bb cornet someone had found in a cupboard somewhere. It was a horrible thing with a great wide mouthpiece but I managed to make it sound all right I think though I knocked a couple of notes over. At least the chaps seemed to think so! I played Schubert's Ave Maria to finish and when I looked out there were tears and not just from the nurses I can tell you! (Perhaps my playing was that bad!)

Things are still fairly quiet here though we can hear our brave guns firing more frequently now, though still quite far away. The ones near us still lie silent again for now and ours is a life of luxury compared to what some fellows are having these days.

I hope this finds you well my darling family. Don't worry about me, I am in high spirits and have made some topping new pals out here. There is nothing to worry about in fact as the Frenchies say, 'San Fairy Anne!"

The only thing I want for is chocolate and socks, so Ma! …………..!

Your loving son ,Harry

What he didn't mention was that Corporal Fox had sat staring at him from two rows back throughout the entire performance, mouthing obscenities in an attempt to put him off. There was no way of understanding why he still felt the need to hurt him and Harry didn't try. He hardly ever saw him and out in France his bullying hurt less than it had at home though it was still unpleasant.

The letter that reached him two weeks later was full of exciting news. His Ma had started working at Vickers steel works making munitions. The work was exhausting and her skin had taken on a strange yellow hue due to the strong chemicals she was handling but she told Harry she was happy to be doing her bit. "They call us the canary girls and we're finally proving that we women are equal to any men here!" The most exciting section though was from his father. He was among a group of men from Ecclesfield tasked with patrolling at night watching for zeppelins in the skies over Sheffield. Since the terrible attacks where the giant airships had bombed London and towns on the Norfolk coast Sheffield people were convinced their great steel- producing city, which was so vital to England's war effort would be next. Even more exciting for Harry though was the news that William Green and Company were being commandeered for the making of steel armour plate for ships and women were to be employed so the remaining men who were of the right age could be released to fight. "I could be out there with you before Christmas if it lasts that long and then you can be proud of your old Pa at last!"

"Hey up Houdini! Good news? You look like the cat that got the cream," said Corporal Croggan emerging from a dugout where he'd been to scrounge some tobacco from the officers.

"Looks like my pa will be allowed to do his bit soon after all," Harry grinned

"Well that's grand lad, good luck to him, from what I hear we're going to need all the men we can get."

CHAPTER FIFTEEN:

Late August 1915

On the twenty fifth of August 1915 the war suddenly became terrifyingly real for Harry and his pals out at the front. They had spent four more days in the front-line trenches and were back in billets at the farm again when there was a big push to drive the Germans back further down the line and the guns had opened up from both sides. Huddled in forward trenches the men had endured days and nights of unrelenting, ear splitting explosions and the scream and crump of the shells that ripped the air as they flew their deadly missions. Attempts to go over the top at intervals along a great waving front line had been an appalling failure as the Allied shells had fallen short of the German lines so their barbed wire was intact and their machine gun emplacements were untouched. The men walked in their hundreds into raking fire which simply mowed them down. The offensive was a terrible disaster and on a sunny afternoon the wounded began to arrive at the field hospital. There were hundreds; some walking but with bandages covering their eyes.

"Gas," muttered John-Willy Sprake when Harry asked him what had happened, but the vast majority were simply laid out on stretchers in the field until beds could be allocated. Some were rushed straight into the tents which were kitted out as operating theatres where ghastly operations to save, but change their lives forever were hurriedly carried out. That night as Harry lay in his blanket trying to sleep, their moans and calls for their mothers haunted him. Their grey faces and blank staring eyes, shocked beyond expression turned towards his mind's eye and he cried. This was no "big picnic" no "show" no "great game". For the first time since the moment a bullet had nearly killed him, Harry was afraid, terribly afraid. He tried to force his mind to think of the fields and woods of home, arguments and play fights with his beloved Laurie, the funny way Frank spoke, Douglas's serious face and clips round the ear from his Ma for being cheeky, but they wouldn't come. The roar of the guns, relentless and terrifying and the bewildered faces of the young men who had been sent in under them filled every atom of his being. He knew his turn was creeping towards him relentless and unstoppable like a dirty wave. Somewhere, drinking port in a chateau, miles behind the lines generals were poring over maps and calculating how many men they could afford to lose to gain a few hundred yards of territory. They were trying to guess the weather conditions so they could launch gas attacks with a minimal risk of the wind changing direction and sending it back into the faces of their own men and pretending to themselves that the war was being won despite the terrible carnage. Because he'd been told to, Harry tried to hate the Germans but he couldn't do that either. He didn't know them and all he had experienced of them were the strange guttural shouts he'd heard drifting across no-man's land from their trenches just a hundred yards or so away when he was in the line or what was even worse their lovely tuneful singing. How could you hate a choir of young men? They were just more men. Men who died just as easily as English men. Men who got letters from home, had mothers and fathers and sweethearts, brothers, sisters and children. Men who probably didn't understand this war any more than he did. Men who took the time to make plangent, sweet music. In another life Fritz and Tommy could have just been funny nicknames between friends. He became aware of a little figure silhouetted in the doorway of the barn against the orange glow of the muzzle blast of the guns. The red dot of a glowing cigarette moved periodically up and down. Corporal Croggan had cadged another fag from someone and was looking over his beloved lads as they settled down to try and sleep.

A faint silver mist cloaked the dewy fields around the farm as Harry blew the first note of reveille and a deer, startled as it fed in a low hedgerow jerked its head up and gazed, stock still, its black muzzle shiny in the early morning light. It was a roe with two little prong horns and it was in its red summer coat and even as he played amid the madness of war Harry found himself thinking it was beautiful and he envied the simplicity of its life. It snorted two tiny smoky plumes, stamped a foreleg and in one enormous bound, cleared the hedge and was gone. The guns had fallen silent again in this section. They spread more terror at night, and the men of the battery who were utterly exhausted were just trudging back to billets, hollow eyed and muttering. Their replacements would start again and fire unexpectedly and intermittently through the day but for now these men were out of it. One raised a weary hand to Harry but most simply stared ahead or at the ground as they stumbled to their rest. It had been a bad show.

"That's the ticket laddie!" Captain Gregg called as he emerged from the farm house where the officers were billeted, "Top brass coming today." He turned and called to a rigidly saluting man nearby, "Let's have the chaps up and looking their best Sergeant Major Blackwell," then to Harry, "Blow it again young bugler!" In the past few weeks the officers had become much closer to the men they were commanding. There was a spirit of, "all in this together" though they were billeted and messed separately.

Blackwell was standing on the area that had been designated as the parade ground for the men before Harry had even emerged from his billet and played the first note. He was a frightening figure with cropped red hair, a closely clipped moustache, small, glittering, ice blue eyes and the straightest back Harry had ever seen in his life. He seemed never to rest and gave of an aura of indestructability and utter fearlessness which meant that the men hated him and admired him equally.

"Do as the officer commanded lad, on the double!" he yelled and Harry made an utter hash of repeating reveille as his hands were shaking so much.

Blackwell tried to hide a smile as he turned away but Harry distinctly saw his eyes twinkle and his moustache twitch.

"Rotten bugger, he did that on purpose!" he muttered to himself as he slung his bugle back across his chest and headed across to the long line of canvas sinks ranged outside the barn where all the other men were beginning to wash and shave, grumbling and jostling and rubbing the sleep from their eyes.

CHAPTER SIXTEEN:

September 1915

The cavalry officers arrived just after two o clock on a September afternoon when the men had been mercilessly drilled by Blackwell for two hours in the heat of the day. Their great stamping, snorting horses were burnished like conkers and the haughty men astride them wore the cleanest, neatest uniforms the men had ever seen. Their sabres, slung low in polished steel scabbards glinted in the sunshine clattering against the horses' tack as they wheeled and stamped raising a great choking cloud of yellow dust.

"'Ere they come," said Sam out of the side of his mouth. He was standing at attention next to Harry and risking a monumental shouting at by Blackwell for talking on parade. "Look at 'em! Useless load of buggers that lot! Try doing a cavalry charge across no- man's land, they'd just get going and they'd tipple into a trench! Just look at the swagger of 'em, if they don't stop careering about Fritz won't have to send any more gas over, all this dust'll choke us to death."

Harry was saved from having to risk a dangerous reply by the arrival, amidst a great deal of shouting by the cavalry officers of a grand staff car in which sat a small red faced man in the uniform of a major general. The three brass studs on his shoulder shone like gold and his Sam Brown was polished to an impossibly high sheen which made it appear to be made of polished rosewood. Captain Greenwood from Harry's battalion stepped forward, opened the car door, stood back and saluted smartly. The general clambered out, giving a lazy salute back then walked towards the hushed men, flanked by Greenwood and the young lieutenant who had said Harry was made of the right stuff. Blackwell stiffened as they approached, saluted and screamed, "Eyes front!" at his troops.

"This is it then," whispered Sam, "the off."

The general's speech after he'd stood them at ease was full of praise for the men who stood before him on that hot afternoon; praise for them and praise for the city of Sheffield which had raised this great battalion. He knew they were tough, brave lads; he knew they were proud and patriotic; he knew they would fight to defend their country and their king and he knew theirs was a righteous cause with God on their side. There was no actual mention of the action to come but the men knew it was coming at last and it would be their show and Harry could sense a ripple of excitement and a straightening of backs and shoulders as they listened. When it was over and the shouts and salutes and clattering of horses and car had receded into the distance Harry blew the dismissal and the men wandered back to billets.

"When do you reckon it'll be Sarn't Major?" asked a pale worried looking private when Blackwell checked on the men later.

"Soon lad, we've orders to go up to the first reserve trenches at dawn on the twentieth, day after tomorrow. It's going to be a big show so write your letters and get as much grub down you as you can, you need to be ready."

There was a gentleness in his voice that Harry had never heard before as it was usually all bully and bluster and bristle and Blackwell stood silently for a moment in the doorway of the barn, looking over them all before he turned smartly on his heel and stalked away.

"Queer old fish isn't he?" Gerald Brightside said to no one in particular but no one answered; they were sunk in their own thoughts.

That night the guns which had been rolled half a mile further towards the front began their deadly barrage in earnest and the air was filled with the great booming roar of the eighteen pounders forming the pounding timpani to a terrible orchestra of screeching Howitzers and banging field guns. Each type of shell made its own distinctive, horrible sound, some whizzed like demented fireworks, others screeched and whistled but the end result was always the same, the dull crump and thud of an explosion of which there were so many and of such frequency that the sound merged into one continuous roaring barrel roll. Over the top could be heard a deadly descant, the clatter and chatter of machine guns and Harry found it difficult to imagine that any living thing could survive amongst the hellish onslaught.

"The lads sent out to check the wire'll be catching it when Fritz joins in," someone said close to Harry but no one else seemed to have heard him among the din, either that or they didn't want to acknowledge that those men were unlikely to be coming back and it was their own turn next.

Harry looked across the barn and was shocked to see Robert Fox sitting hunched on a camp bed in the uniform of a private. He was looking at no one but repetitively picking at the skin around his fingernails, occasionally nibbling a bit off. He was shivering and from time to time appeared to be muttering to himself. His usually mean little eyes looked hollow and wide and Harry thought he looked ill. He'd obviously been demoted from his rank of lance corporal which was no real surprise but Harry felt no satisfaction, instead he felt pity for the sad, unhappy young soldier who seemed so diminished. He didn't feel the urge to approach him however and turned to writing a letter amid the din of the pounding artillery fire. It was not an easy letter to write. He didn't want to alarm his beloved family but he couldn't hide the fact that his platoon would soon be going into action with all the terror that entailed. In the end, he opted for the light-hearted soldiers' banter that men used to take the sting out of the awful reality. He wrote of the "show" they were to take part in and how the Boche would "scarper like rats" when they "copped a packet from old Tommy Atkins". He assured them he would come on all right and see them after it was over but his hand shook and his heart said something different as he signed off, "Yours, your loving son and brother, Harry"

The rain fell like daggers of ice all night as Harry and the rest of his platoon cowered in the bottom of a crumbling trench under the howling horror shredding the sky overhead. From time to time when the enemy found their range a shell would burst on the parapet and they were showered with a pattering rain of mud and stones that clattered on their helmets like enormous hail, got in their eyes and clogged their nostrils. This was the third day they had spent waiting. At night men were sent out on patrol to make gaps in their own barbed wire and assess the state of the German wire; some were left hanging on that wire like pathetic, ragged scarecrows having drawn machine gun fire. John Fenwick was one of them.

Harry glanced around. In the flaring greenish glow of Verey Lights he saw faces that were hardly recognisable, smeared in mud but stark white and drawn with wide eyes and clenched teeth. The officers were doing their best, moving quietly among the men, patting a shoulder here, speaking quietly reassuring words there, trying to smile, telling their chaps they were brave; the best; the only ones for the job they were going to have to do when the time came. Sam beckoned Harry over. He was sucking ferociously on a gasper, jetting the smoke out of his nostrils in an almost continuous stream.

"All right son?"

Harry could only nod. He concentrated on trying to stop his teeth from chattering and force a smile. His head was full of his mam and dad and their Laurie whose faces he was struggling to conjure. They kept swimming into clarity but before he could grasp them and make them stay, the rolling drumfire and sudden explosions would make them snap out of focus and become misty ghosts.

"Bit scared," he replied, "we're close aren't we?"

"Aye we are Harry lad, we're in it up to us necks so we have to do the best we can."

"When do you reckon it'll be?"

"Word is t'day after tomorrow. Barrage should have done for most of 'em and their wire'll be down by then so there shouldn't be owt to stop us."

Harry tried to believe him but the shells and machine guns continued to tell a different story. Corporal Croggan came around a corner of the trench, his helmet jammed down and his coat collar turned up against the rain. "Jones! I've been looking for you son, come with me, Captain Greenwood wants to see you at the double." He looked sharply at Harry with his little, glittering dark eyes. "Come on Houdini, let's see if your escape skills can help you here!"

The dugout was dimly lit by candles standing in mess tins and the air inside was thick with pipe smoke. With every great thudding explosion, little trickles of sandy earth and tiny pinkling pebbles fell from the roof. Captain Greenwood looked up from a sheaf of papers on the table where he sat as Harry and Croggan ducked through the low doorway.

"Ah! Bugler! In you come laddy. All right corporal, dismissed."

Croggan winked at Harry, saluted smartly and ducked back out into the deafening roar of the bombardment.

"Now then bugler I need to ask you a question," said Greenwood, looking keenly at Harry's face. "I fancy you're a little young for this lot?"

Harry hesitated then said stoutly, "No sir, I just look it, all my family's little; my pa's only five foot three." The lie had been repeated so often that it slipped out as smooth as an eel but Harry didn't meet Greenwood's eyes and the officer picked up on it and gave a gentle smile.

"You know of course that our show is imminent?"

"Yes sir, all the men are saying so, they reckon day after tomorrow."

"Yes, well it's no secret any more, I have the orders here," he said, "the men will be told in the next few minutes but I don't want you in it. You're underage, you shouldn't be here so I'm going to send you back to rest. Of course, your papers tell a different story so I'm on a sticky wicket."

A vision of his father hunched over the dining table staring at a white feather swam into Harry's mind, "Don't do that sir, I'll do my bit, I won't let you down!" Greenwood squeezed his tired eyes with thumb and forefinger before looking directly at the little lad standing stiffly before him. This was all wrong he'd hardly lived yet. Harry was about to speak again but his words were drowned by a terrific explosion which brought a shower of earth and stones tumbling down followed a few seconds later by the cries and shouts of injured men.

"Very well private," said Captain Greenwood jamming his steel helmet on and heading for the doorway to assess the casualties, "have it your way, just have that bugle ready and listen for orders; it might be the only thing we can hear in this bloody row."

And he was gone.

CHAPTER SEVENTEEN:

September 1917

Twenty-one year-old Captain Simon Greenwood was thinking of his sweetheart Sally Downing. They had hastily become engaged six months ago and he had only seen her twice since that happy day. The letter he was finishing was the most difficult he'd ever had to write because in it he had to tell her how much he loved her but also be heartbreakingly honest about the perils of the coming day. He knew full well that as an officer he was expected to lead his men calmly over the top bearing only a revolver and his swagger stick. He told Sally of his trust in his men and his pride in leading them and how he felt the weight of responsibility to send them back safely to their sweethearts and families just as he would return to her. He couldn't explain it but somehow the love he felt for this scruffy, vulgar, funny bunch of men under his command would drive him forward into whatever hell the enemy had waiting in store for them. Call it honour or destiny or duty but beneath those words was love and fierce loyalty. His privileged background and private education meant nothing now on this day when the test was the same for all men. The town of Loos-en-Gohelle, if it could be captured from the Germans, might open up the war and end the stalemate. It lay a few tantalising kilometres behind the German trenches and provided the enemy wire had been destroyed and the machine gun nests obliterated by British artillery as promised, it should just be a matter of walking across the open fields, capturing the enemy trenches and pushing them back beyond the town. At least that's what Greenwood wrote to his sweetheart in the dim, pearly light of the growing dawn.

"I have the men assembled sir!" came a harsh voice. Sergeant Blackwell had come into the dug-out and was standing stiffly to attention, his saluting right hand quivering and his black-bright boots gleaming in the candle light.

"As you were Sergeant Major Blackwell. Ten minutes to zero, I shall be there in two minutes, go back and join the men." Then as Blackwell turned he added, "You must show me how to get a shine on my boots like that if we come through."

"Be a pleasure sir, spit, that's the secret!"

"Right-o, jolly good, I'll remember that."

"Pleasure sir, good luck. See you on the other side."

There was twenty years between them but the sergeant had a glowing respect for the young officer who had proved himself utterly fearless since he'd been in command, leading raiding parties and night patrols over and over, always at the front and never shirking.

"Yes, Blackwell. Good luck. God save the jolly old king and all that," he added with a grin. Blackwell was a fierce royalist and Captain Greenwood enjoyed teasing him gently by being flippant; perhaps this would be his last opportunity.

"If I may say sir, you're a damned disgrace to the uniform," Blackwell countered with a wink and a flash of a grin.

"Get out Sergeant Major before my Bolshevik tendencies get the better of me."

Blackwell saluted again and left the young captain to seal his letter and prepare himself for the battle ahead.

Harry was standing in the lee of the trench wall with the rest of his section listening to the scream and boom of the final bombardment. The men were mainly silent, some smoking, some mouthing prayers and silent mantras to themselves, each a little island yet staunchly together. Harry was thinking again of his ma and pa and their Laurie. All he wanted now was to make them proud. His pa would be joining up any day now and Harry was imagining a Christmas on leave where the two of them stood in The Black Bull in uniform together bellowing out carols as the snow fell. His bugle hung on its silken cord across his chest and he ran his fingers over its smooth cold curves and pictured his soprano cornet in its velvet nest again just waiting for him at home on the whatnot in his bedroom.

"Zero hour in two minutes, lads. Final checks. We're sending gas over so make sure your gas helmets are at the top of your packs in case of a change of wind direction." As the officer spoke, the men heard the soft whizz and hoot of eighteen pounder gas shells amongst the roar and crash of the bombardment, then suddenly profound silence.

The barrage was over so it was almost time.

Greenwood looked at his beloved lads then took out a pocket watch.

"Good luck! Remember to hold formation and Houdini, stay close to me. Orders are to press forward come what may but I may need you to signal," he said, then placed a silver whistle between his lips and put one foot on the bottom rung of the trench ladder wedged against the parapet.

He watched the second-hand track inexorably upwards and when it reached the top he blew as hard as he could and began to climb. All along the trench came the shrill of whistles and men began to scramble upwards and over the crumbling parapet. Harry had half expected battle cries and noise but it was almost silent but for the scuffle of boots and the odd grunt of effort. His mentor and friend Sam was next to go. He turned his white face to Harry and managed a wink before scrambling up and disappearing over the lip of the trench. Harry clambered after him feeling the weight of his heavy pack dragging at him as he climbed, then he was over and walking across a field hung over with the morning's first singing larks where wisps of mist still clung to the ruined ground colourful with patches of poppies. He glanced left to make sure he was close to Captain Greenwood and saw the officer striding bolt upright with his revolver held before him and his swagger stick under his arm. Men were looking left and right grinning at each other. Perhaps the promises were right. Perhaps Fritz was done for and their trenches were destroyed.

"Hold the line! Keep formation!" Sergeant Blackwell's voice came clear and strong from Harry's right, "Steady as you go!"

There was a dreamlike quality to this strange, silent, waking landscape after the days of noise and stink and Harry felt as though he were cocooned in a little pocket of quiet where the ground was rolling backwards under him and he was watching the world as if he were separate and not part of it. His feet were moving automatically and he was keeping the line but it felt unreal and oddly calm.

The line had gone two hundred yards when the first shells landed and the machine guns began to clatter. The enemy lines were intact, their rolls of barbed wire were unbroken; the bombardment had fallen short. Men to left and right began to fall and stumble, some simply sank silently, some cried out and struggled. Harry felt the reality surge back with a sickening jolt and his legs turned to watery jelly as the terrifying roar of falling shells and the singing whistle of fragments of hot metal filled the air. Great plumes of black earth rose from the ground mixed with hideous yellow smoke and stinking Lyddite and the air moved in great chunks of concussion that pushed him backwards and sideways. All around him men were flung like broken dolls or simply disappeared in the flash and thud of explosions. Yet still Harry stumbled onwards. As far as he knew his Captain was still to his left and he had been ordered to stay close. He peered right. A grim faced Corporal Croggan peered back through the smoke and flying earth, his mouth working silent words, his knuckles white as he held his bayonetted rifle before him. Then suddenly he stopped. His face registered resignation for a moment then he pitched forward onto his face in the mud. The horror and grief would have to wait. Harry's blind instinct carried him on until suddenly he was aware of a voice screaming.

"For Christ's sake blow the retreat bugler! We're being cut to ribbons!" It was Blackwell who'd broken ranks and was weaving towards Harry skirting shell holes and ducking each time there was a deafening explosion. Harry looked left. Greenwood was shouting something but his words were lost in the tumult and suddenly he was gone seemingly evaporating in the hot blast and thump of a direct hit. The shock wave tumbled Harry backwards and earth smashed into his face, filling his nostrils and eyes. He lay, stunned and deafened, unable to breathe after the hammer blow to his body and the battle seemed to pause around him until his senses flooded back and clawing feebly at the soft black earth, he dragged himself onto his front and began to suck air in again. For a few seconds, he was aware only of the awful scratching pain of the mud in his eyes and he pawed it away, blinking and snuffling and half crying as the din of the battle came back in a muffled roar. When he could see, he realised he was in the bottom of a deep shell hole. His bugle was still grasped tightly in his hand because he had been about to follow Sergeant Blackwell's screamed order. He dragged himself into a sitting position and through bleary eyes looked around him. With a shock, he realised there was a huddled figure crouching on the far side of the shell crater. He was crushed sideways on to the crater wall and at first Harry thought he must be dead as he was in such a strange position but then he saw that the man had his hands pressed to his mouth and was gnawing at them.

"Hello!" Harry shouted. His voice sounded odd inside his head as though he had his fingers pressed hard into his ears and he realised the absurdity of what he had said, almost as though he was calling across the cow field to one of his mates.

The figure showed no sign of having heard so Harry began to crawl towards him. His face was turned away and there was a patch of blood on his shoulder. He was very thin and his uniform seemed to be wrapped around him rather than worn by him.

"Hey," Harry said, reaching out and touching the bony shoulder, "Hey!"

The haunted eyes that turned towards him were Robert Fox's

"I want my mam." A harsh whisper.

Harry had no words.

"I want my mam, I want my mam, I want my mam."

Harry shuffled until he could get an arm round Foxy's shoulder and ease him gently away from the crater side. One side of his face was black with mud and his lips were drawn back over chattering teeth.

"I want my mam, where's my mam? I want her."

Harry didn't know what to say so he cuddled Foxy closer and stroked his hair. Somewhere the older boy had lost his helmet. Words came then, "It'll be all right Foxy, we'll find your mam." He realized he had never known Robert Fox's mam and wondered when the last time Robert had seen her was. As far as he knew Foxy had been just a little lad when she disappeared from his life and his drunken bullying father had been left to bring him up.

"I want my mam, I want my mam." His voice was little and panicky and he chewed at the back of his knuckles drawing blood. Another great explosion rent the air showering the two boys with earth and stones and Robert Fox twitched and squirmed in Harry's arms. He began to cry.

"IwantmymamIwantmymamIwantmymam."

The words came in a constant stream now and Harry had to hold him very tight to stop him breaking away. "We'll find her Robert, we'll find her, she'll come soon, just try and be still." Suddenly the older boy went silent and slumped against Harry's chest sobbing and snuffling. It was just a moment but Harry relaxed his grip and Robert Fox broke free and scrambled up the side of the shell hole. Harry grabbed for his ankle but it was too late. He was up and over and running towards the terrible hail of machine gun bullets crying for his mother. Harry scrambled after him then did the only thing he could think of. Standing on the lip of the crater he stood upright, raised his bugle to his lips and blew the retreat as hard as he could. The piercing notes cut through the din of battle and the last thing Harry saw before the bullets hit him was Robert Fox stopping and turning as he instinctively obeyed the bugle's call and headed for safety. Harry never felt himself falling forward, crushing his bugle beneath his chest. Nor did he feel the huge explosion before a great cresting wave of earth buried him.

In Ecclesfield his pa proudly signed a piece of paper, his left hand on the bible.

CHAPTER EIGHTEEN:
2016

"……..At the going down of the sun and in the morning we will remember them."

Mr Jones' voice faltered a little on the last few words of the famous poem and the children remained solemnly still for a few moments after he finished.

"Please stay where you are, there's one more thing before you go," Chris, the guide said gently.

Through the small iron gate a figure was striding. He was in the immaculate uniform of The Yorkshire Regiment and after marching smartly past the huddled group of children he stamped to attention facing them across the sad, snow covered mound of the little grave. He raised a gleaming bugle on a silken cord to his lips and the clean, pure notes of the Last Post rang out for Harry Jones.

Printed in Great Britain
by Amazon